Y E

O F

W E D N E S D A Y S

*May all your encounters
be magical ones*

Sonia Bahl

Sonia Bahl

FiNGERPRINT!

Published by

FiNGERPRINT!

An imprint of Prakash Books India Pvt. Ltd.

113/A, Darya Ganj, New Delhi-110 002,
Tel: (011) 2324 7062 – 65, Fax: (011) 2324 6975
Email: info@prakashbooks.com/sales@prakashbooks.com

facebook www.facebook.com/fingerprintpublishing
twitter www.twitter.com/FingerprintP
www.fingerprintpublishing.com

ISBN: 978 93 8881 065 4

Processed & printed in India

Puneet

My true north

Zara, Sunay, Amev

My east, my west, my south

Acknowledgement

Full disclosure. This, the second novel, was never meant to happen. Not on the cards. Wasn't planned. I lacked the requisite great author-ish ambitions. My day job is writing movies. I am busy and deluded enough to be happy with that. Besides, as I asked the editor (of my debut novel) when she suggested I get started on my next one, "Who wants to read more of what I have to say?" The response was stunning in its specificity: "I do." Well, I thought, at least I'd know my target audience: Pooja Dadwal—Commissioning Editor at Fingerprint! Publishing. One could not ask for a better collaborator. Hyper-intelligent, relentlessly demanding, deeply receptive, and endlessly patient with my linguistic shortcomings. And yet I remained inert to her request until I began receiving not-so-subtle text reminders, nudging me to share *just one page* of the story that she was sure I had written in my head.

And that's how it began. One line, one page, and then one chapter—via WhatsApp! It was more like a: there, happy now? She wasn't. "I *need* to know what happens next. Can you please just finish it?"

Thank you, Pooja. *A Year of Wednesdays* is as much yours as it's mine.

Mita Kapur, my literary agent, and the whole team at Fingerprint! Publishing—you've been championing my cause ever since I dared to stray into the publishing world. I am truly grateful.

A massive shout-out to Chaitanya Hegde and Datta Dave—the men behind Tulsea Talent, my managers in this mad adventure called screenwriting. All writing! You don't just provide the air cover, and make sure I do the work I love to do, you believe in what I do. The best part: you've never once stepped back when I've politely requested for the impossible.

This public acknowledgement of gratitude would be woefully incomplete without thanking my first reader and annoyingly sharp proofreader of all that I write—even a grocery list. Downside: he's terrifyingly transparent and unabashedly critical. Upside: he's embarrassingly supportive—cheerleading is his resting pulse. He's also my husband. So, laughing through my bruised ego sulks is par for the course.

Sonia Bahl

A Wednesday

I magine being squeezed into an airplane toilet with two other people. A man whom you've never met until an hour ago and a fourteen-month-old baby who needs his diaper changed.

If I had a list titled 'Possible Scenarios That Would Never Happen To Me', this moment would jostle for top slot. Even though there is a perfectly logical explanation for how I got here.

They say the hospitality of people in Delhi can kill you. I am (barely) living proof of that at the end of every single trip I make to the city. This time the effects have been dramatically compounded owing to the fact that it was a seven-day trip for a five-day wedding celebration. As an NRI with an underwhelming digestive track record, I tend to start off by being vigilant and cautious of my intake, but then greed and susceptibility to pampering trump all good sense, and I'm wolfing down everything—gloriousness that finds its way to me through deep-fried fare, chaat dunked in yoghurt laced with lethal chutneys, ghee-soaked sweets (moong dal halwa? Why not!)—faster than the attendees at an ancient Rome food orgy.

No, it never ends well.

Before leaving for the airport I am usually seen knocking back Imodium and anti-nausea tablets—with the urgency of an addict, might I add—to plug me up for life.

Wait, I've been so busy trumpeting my dubious achievements, did I mention that the fourteen-month-old in question is mine? Carrying a chubby toddler, after surrendering his stroller for security reasons, feels like carrying Vin Diesel (with his full set of dumb-bells), especially if you haven't eaten all day. And that insignificantly short walk from the gate through the aerobridge to your seat feels like Mandela's *Long Walk to Freedom*—minus the resilience, grace, and innate dignity associated with it. And when you're feeling like a sullen, underfed supermodel minus the looks, even a business class seat feels painfully small. First class, you ask? Frankly, even a full suite doesn't cut it.

At that point, which was almost an hour ago, the only viable fantasy in my head was to ditch commercial and opt for a private jet. Although, if the seat next to mine could somehow stay vacant I promised myself to feel more asset rich than Richard Branson and every person who worked for his airline.

A few minutes later a man sauntered in. Tall, sharp-suited, designer stubble, and a head of just-shampooed perfectly coiffed hair. Was it my own energy-depleted, diarrhoea-plugged state that made him appear fresher and smoother than he really was? Or was he really an athlete at his peak, modelling an expensive suit? The same one who had just shot up a dose of performance-enhancing drugs? How else could anyone look so spa-energized and relaxed-fit for a post-midnight long-haul flight? Well, that was until he noticed his neighbours, my son and me. Then he looked like someone who had just glimpsed his own slow death. Next came a polite grimace masquerading as a smile. And he was gone! Just like that. Truth be told, most sensible people would disembark from a moving plane, at high altitude, to avoid sitting near an infant and his presently-not-fit-for-consumption mother. Luckily for athletic guy, we were still parked on the runway.

Finally, the doors closed, the crew started buzzing through the aisles, and the cabin transformed into a beehive of take-off activity. He wasn't back. My baby nodded off to sleep and the world was near-perfect. I glanced at the empty seat next to me and started to feel decidedly Bransonesque. But just as the seat belt signs came on, the man came back. This time in grey jogging pants caught at the bottom, dropped at the crotch, formal Oxfords swapped for Toms, a perfectly un-ironed white round neck tee, and holding the erstwhile worn suit in a Louis Vuitton suit bag. Maybe athletic guy was actually a bona fide member of Tom Ford's squad. Great. I was going to neighbour with Mr GQ whilst dabbing drool and throw up off my sweater and fervently praying my baby didn't drop an outrageously smelly poop in his diaper during take-off. Well, it's fifteen hours and thirty minutes, how bad could things get?

Once Tom Ford neighbour was seated, he lifted his partition like he'd just resurrected the Berlin Wall and if I trespassed there could be blood. Warning heeded. Not by baby, though, who stood up after a brief nap and looked like he might consider knocking down the sacred barrier between eye-masked, headphoned, pointedly-blocking-the-world-out neighbour and us. No! He was exactly the kind of person one didn't do that to. He was going to be acutely unimpressed by any and all of the baby antics and most of all by ones that invaded his privacy, space, and sound. Any minute now he might shrivel us to cinders with one perfectly shaped eyebrow raised in disapproval.

Thankfully, God and cold medication work in mysterious ways. Within minutes, baby had a change of heart—called off his plans for a surgical strike, curled up in my lap, and nodded off to sleep. As did I. Only to be jolted awake by exceptionally bad weather thirty minutes later. Not bad as in mild turbulence from the usual air pockets. But deep nosedives like the pilot had opted for a kamikaze flight pattern. There was lots of throw up—miraculously none of it from my baby—and percussive buzzing for the crew. By which time I concluded my baby was born to spend his entire life on the nausea and vertigo inducing Space Mountain theme park ride. He hadn't stirred even once through the blood-curdling moments when we *knew* we were going to morph from real people into aviation statistics.

I, on the other hand, had passed out for a bit. Now, I'm not a skittish flyer, never have been, so it had to have been that stomach bug. Although it's a moot point when you've just handed your toddler to Neighbour over his Berlin Wall, seconds before blissfully fainting. I'd like to call it pure mother's instinct—handing over baby safely first, then collapsing. Something told me Neighbour was more likely to call it non-invasive vasectomy. The type that automatically fixes any notions he might have nurtured about procreating.

Thankfully, I came around a few minutes later and was terribly relieved to note Mr GQ hadn't tossed my son out of the window, but was, in fact, holding him, albeit like one might have held a giant soiled diaper.

A flight attendant rushed past me before I could articulate the word 'help'. Apparently, there were more than several acutely sick passengers on board. She was followed by two more attendants who looked like participants in an ill-timed relay, one of whom stopped in response to a weak wave from me. She helpfully thrust a glass of sugary water into my clammy hands, insisting I needed to up my energy. There was an eighty-year-old who needed resuscitating, she told me, imparting this information in a manner that made me feel guilty for merely passing out.

I noticed Neighbour had lowered his partition and was looking politely at me. I looked back equally politely—the decent neighbourly thing to do. Oh, of course, he was holding my son! Who was now wide awake and reasonably comfortable despite being held at a somewhat safe distance from Neighbour's body.

"Barf bag?" I heard him say.

Now that might seem like a perfectly civil, even considerate question to those who couldn't see his superior, unflappable face, but to me it distinctly felt like he was letting me know what he thought of me. Despite what appeared to be a snarky put-down, I managed a reasonably cheerful response. "No thanks. I mean thanks for holding him . . . but I'm absolutely fine now."

He handed over my son, and dear God, how could something so small smell like the rear of a full-sized garbage truck? Neighbour reached for his headphones, looking at me with an exotic cocktail of mock sympathy, pity, and—was that a dash of unmasked disdain? "Intense, yeah?" One last superior smile and he went back to doing what people without babies on planes did: watching the latest action movie without a care in the world. While I began to prepare for full-on combat.

Armed with diaper bag on one shoulder and baby on the other, I got up to head to the toilet, just one thought running on loop in my head: *let the toilet with a changing table be vacant. Let the toilet with a changing table be vacant.* You see, it is hell without a changing table. But it is lower than the Mariana Trench when you're feeling woozy and have no changing table.

At that exact moment the pilot decided to do a belly-up flip, or maybe I was dizzy again. Everyone around me looked fine, so it was definitely a little spin of vertigo. Either way, I couldn't decide if I was more anxious about dropping my helpless toddler or about having smug Neighbour toss me yet another you-barf-bag look. What he did, though, took the narrative right out of my hands, into completely unexpected, unanticipated territory.

"The crew is going nuts, so you're not going to get much help. If you're still feeling sick, I could wait outside the washroom . . . Yeah?"

He enunciated the word 'outside' with zealous clarity. Roger that—got it, loud and clear. And yet it was an offer I couldn't scoff at. I snapped it up while making an impassioned promise to the universe never to judge sartorially superior looking people. Ever again.

The two vacant toilets had no changing table. The third one did. Only problem was, it had gotten locked and jammed during the turbulence and the crew didn't look like they were going to get to it any time soon. Neighbour pushed back his sleeves and looked like a man ready to climb Everest, minus any climbing equipment. "Okay, let's do this," he said.

Anyone who's ever changed a baby's diaper in an airplane toilet minus a changing table deserves to be inducted into the Navy SEALs. Really. This was how we went about it: Neighbour held baby facing me and stopped breathing. I peeled off the soiled diaper—careful not to spill its anaesthetizing contents—put half a dozen wet wipes to their best use, and secured a fresh diaper on baby. All done with such virtuoso precision, speed, and robotic efficiency that in those moments, we could have put the *Titanic* back to its original state while simultaneously saving every person on board. Admittedly, the speed, high concentration levels, and acute lack of space left me feeling somewhat light-headed, while Neighbour looked positively breathless. Neighbour's expensive cologne—were those mint undertones?—fought valiantly but failed to drown the powerful odour from the job at hand. Thankfully, in less than three minutes, we had baby changed, smelling sweet, and our hands washed. Not to put too fine a point on it, helpful Neighbour ensured his hands were scrubbed, in excruciatingly paranoid fashion.

Watching the flag flyer of urbane coolness examine his scrubbed hands brought on a fresh wave of mortification. How had something like this just happened between *this* person and us? Were we simply hapless victims of some grand cosmic clerical error?

***

The plane and my nerves settle into a steady hum. Neighbour is sipping champagne and smiling at his screen. Baby has guzzled his formula milk and is fast asleep on my seat, which is now in flat bed position, but I am sitting up, and get this, browsing the movie titles! World order has been restored.

"Thank you, you were remarkable with him. You probably are or will make a wonderful dad," I say to Neighbour. He stares at me like I am speaking in Latin or perhaps in computer code. That's just fine, I'd also feign selective deafness if I were travelling with me today.

He lifts his headset and waits for me to repeat myself, only to have an even more confusing reaction.

"Oh, holy crap, no! None of that for me." He looks at me like I have just stabbed him with the near-blunt plane cutlery.

I am puzzling over how on earth has my genuine compliment turned into a panic-inducing insult when he leans over and looks at my screen.

"*Jerry Maguire?*" He points at his screen to show me he is watching the same movie. To be fair, the incredulous expression on his face is justified. From over two hundred available titles, how did two people choose the same over-twenty-year-old movie?

"Yeah, it's a classic. Show me the money. Show me the money!" He grins like he's coined the iconic pop culture phrase himself. Of course, that's what appeals to him. Why am I not surprised?

"For me it's about Jerry's heart: the hero's journey, going from the blinkered, aggressive, profit-obsessed sports agent to a man who fights against all odds to reclaim his humanity. To become idealistic and incorruptible." When I finish speaking, he's aglow with satisfaction; I'm guessing from placing a mental check mark over my head: predictable, sanctimonious bore.

"Why am I not surprised?"

He says exactly what I'd felt barely a minute ago but been too polite to articulate. Then he decides to take it one step further.

"Let me guess, like Reneé Zelwegger's character, you only want to be inspired?"

Unchecked impunity or authentic curiosity? It's hard

to tell the difference when the person has an unfairly open smile and unwavering eyes. It's even harder to be flat-out rude to the person who'd just volunteered to get you through a tricky malodorous experience. "Of course, why else would one work?" I reply.

He throws his head back and laughs. "I'm curious, Greenpeace or primary school teacher?"

There isn't an iota of doubt now. I have been slotted and I am falling abysmally short. I am tempted to refrain from replying. Indulge in fanciful lying: I'm a stay-at-home mom who is also a phone-sex provider. Unfortunately, lying never comes on cue or minus the sensation that I might start choking and then asphyxiate.

"I work for a small nature fund." I can see a blurb pop up over his head with the words 'Tree-Hugger' italicized in green.

"Ah, the hero's journey." His tongue is so firmly wedged in his cheek a high leverage industrial plier will prove useless in prying it out.

"Not really. Our work simply involves getting young people to understand and champion the idea of conservation." You judgemental snob, I finish the sentence in my head.

He is about to lift his headset and place it back over his ears, but then decides to let me know: "I'm the other guy. Jerry before the transformation—choosing to be corrupted by the frantic, heartless, contemporary lust for money and power." Said with the smugness of someone who'll be bringing home a year-end bonus that can take care of Third-World debt.

"Oh, Wall Street." I am hoping my deliberate coolness combined with carefully-laced sarcasm might at least perforate his thick skin, but his all-too-quick 'Bingo' implies I have done the exact opposite. I have simply stoked his pride.

The conversation should have ended right there. Me judging him for being the guy who devotes himself to some unattainable goal: a combination of looking like Cristiano Ronaldo, while hoping to sound like a modern-day Gordon Gekko, the fictional Wall Street symbol of unrestrained greed. And him dismissing me as some environment-obsessed, ambition-free, tofu-promoting vegan, stay-at-home-but-not-very-efficient mom. With the added bonus of a drool-stained sweater and bad decision-making from acute sleep deprivation, which the flight had contributed to in a huge measure. But as it turns out, Neighbour and I end up talking for the next fourteen and something hours. Truth be told, not all of it can be categorized as talking. Battling and sparring sound much too civil and a touch too cutesy. So let's call it biting one's tongue in the nick of time and other forms of damage control.

We also eat. We walk through the cabin. He stretches, bending over and touching the floor with terrifying ease. I gimp behind my toddler, up and down the aisle. He shocks me yet again by walking my son up and down the aisle. But mostly we talk. More in under fifteen hours than most people do in fifteen months.

His parents migrated to Canada when he was ten. They bought and ran a small dry cleaning store. He hated school (thanks to his parents' business, he earned the nickname Cleaner Boy), hated suburbia, hated Canada, hated his life. Undergrad was a relief. New York was the best escape plan. Now he's living the life he hadn't dreamed of. What he is really saying is, he's outlived his best dream. And yet, it is said minus conceit, with unadulterated wonder. The exact same wonder on a child's face when he's kneeling by the Christmas tree and discovers Santa actually drained that glass of milk, ate up the cookies, and left him every single present he'd asked for.

"Not one wrong move, then?" His life sounds like a plan devised by McKinsey & Company and executed to perfection by him. I honestly have no idea how that feels.

"Actually, plenty. For starters, I nearly got sacked from my dream job a year after getting it."

He has a story that makes him laugh more than I imagine people like him allow themselves to laugh. He was the junior member of a hedge fund team that had flown in to Beijing to meet with a client who had taken them to a heritage palace for a ceremonial eight-course meal. He and his colleague found seven of the eight courses nauseatingly inedible, so kept sipping the rice wine in guilt and with a sense of nervous over-compensation for their non-Asian palates. Halfway through the meal, they were so wasted they started giggling uncontrollably and wait, that's not even the worst part. They stabbed their chopsticks into their steamed buns, held them high, and announced. 'Hail, Mao Zedong!'

He also wishes the ceilings of planes are fitted with

sleep inducing lighting designed by Philippe Starck and engineered to prevent disruptions to our circadian rhythm.

"Of course. Champagne isn't enough. They owe us designer sleep-inducing aids. Whimsy for the rich." I swear I have no idea where this came from. If you know me at all, you'll put this down to chemically imbalanced knee-jerk reactions.

"Stop being a snob. You're here too, you know."

"I'm the snob?"

"A confused snob. The good life has to come with a disclaimer or with sarcasm. Me, I love the good life—no apologies."

I had noticed.

Till four hours ago he was the guy who looked like he had no idea there was anyone else inhabiting the world except him. He seemed, at best, the living embodiment of the perfect holiday accessory. Now he is doling out funny stories and bantering with a complete stranger, all with the effortless charm of a late-night comedy show host.

"Whenever you feel like criticizing anyone, just remember that all the people in this world haven't had the advantages that you've had."

Gatsby?! The guy with the hanging crotch sweatpants and just shampooed pompadour is quoting from *The Great Gatsby*? "You read." Honestly, I didn't intend for this thought to turn into words.

"And that wasn't condescending at all. Truth is, I don't read. I mean, does online financial news count? And solicitation from Burberry?"

Okay, I deserve that.

"*Gatsby* was high school mandatory reading. Photographic memory helps. Also, I kind of felt I had some Gatsby in me. Get-rich-at-any-cost type of thing—always had that going for me." He smiles sweetly, then asks, "And you have guilt going for you?"

No, I don't! Wait, do I? But that isn't the point. I am tripping over the astonishingly simple realization that a complete, and very unlikely, stranger has just looked past the layers of blanket, clothes, skin, and bones and peered into what may be (the jury is still out) buried inside with the resolute intention of never coming out.

"You strike me as someone who is driven by doing the right thing." He is on a roll.

"And clearly in some galaxy far away and screwed-up, doing the right thing is unacceptable?" I ask him.

"I'm just saying being good can't be the motivation for everything you do. Do it because it feels right, it feels wrong, it feels delicious, it feels fun, it feels—"

"Powerful and greedy?" I'm sorry but he just walked into that, and I probably need that hormone imbalance test at the very earliest.

"Oh yeah, that too."

"Right. Ever think of becoming a life coach?"

He shrugs. "I think it's just so dull if being good is the only thing you're driven by."

"And you are not presumptuous at all."

You can never seriously argue with a stranger because the stakes are not high enough. You aren't responsible for being responsible. Or for being the person they think you should be (without ever checking with you). Or the one they'd want to change (again, without ever checking with you). That privilege is reserved for the ones we live with and intend to, for the rest of our lives. The same ones we will ascribe all our joys and more particularly, all our tears to, and then inevitably say to them on a bad day, 'It's all your fault'. So when you disagree with a stranger who has the ability to get under your skin, it becomes banter. Banter is supposedly skin-deep and enticingly recreational. But if it slips into the right rhythm it can be dangerous. Sometimes it lingers. It keeps you on edge. It becomes that sensation that lives just outside of your own skin. And it opens up boxes that haven't had their contents aired in a long time. Or, perhaps, ever.

At one point we both are trying to lose ourselves, on separate screens, in the towering narcissism of Jerry Maguire and mid-flight catering. "You're vegetarian. Of course, you are," I hear him say. What kind of person doesn't ask but looks repeatedly amused by what he presumes are your sub-optimal life choices?

"And you, I'm guessing, have your Newport steak butcher's number tattooed on your arm." The unrecognizable new me is now responding with verbal missiles and a complete disregard for politeness.

"Right, right, and a tad wrong."

Said like an annoying game show host revelling in holding all the answers, while you're the contestant who just isn't smart enough to win the big game prize. It isn't discovering that he is a meat-snob carnivore that is the problem. It is how you can knock him on the head with irony and it will go unnoticed, ricochet off his perfect head of hair, and land too far off the mark to have even the slightest impact. Obviously, it doesn't matter that I haven't asked him to elaborate on his coded response; he is going to anyway.

"I do love the Florence Meat Market's Newport steak. I do have a tattoo. But it isn't my butcher's number. It's something else."

I am trying to finish my non-sweetened yoghurt—my first (semi) solid meal in what feels like years. Maybe, it is the lack of nutrients in my body, but the only words that pop into my head and out of my mouth before I can wipe the sarcasm off of them are, "Dollar signs?" And here's the unsettling truth. He doesn't laugh out loud or look incredulous or even mildly offended. He simply elaborates with the eagerness of an intern making his first PowerPoint presentation.

"Dollar signs in the form of a philosophy."

It takes me some recovering and concentration to form the next sentence in my head. "Please tell me you're not even in the vicinity of serious."

In response he lifts his still pristine, still perfectly crushed white tee (that has to be woven with a thread count of one billion and God's own beard) and reveals a washboard for a stomach on which the words *What's the point of fuck you money if you never say fuck you?* are emblazoned in black ink, curving from his navel around to his back.

"Words from a random TV show? Branded into your skin for posterity?"

He grins like I am the one who doesn't get it. I am the one who needs to be roasted. "A show you've clearly watched."

I shake my head so vigorously that my little Space Mountain trooper jolts awake, blinks in a confused manner, but thankfully shows no interest in keeping his eyes open. I pat him gently while I struggle to find some semblance of a suitable response. "I'm aware of the show, but it's a show. Last time I checked, a tattoo is kind of permanent."

It is so simple to write him off as a standard-issue man-child backslapping himself for everything he is and has. To see the strutting pride from being part of a high-octane high-rewards career and marvel at his reverberating shallowness. To wonder how a grown man can adopt over-the-top pop culture references and make them his living, breathing guiding lights. To imagine him as someone who's likely to take his cue from them and in a rush of post-snorting euphoria proudly list out his *Wolf of Wall Street*-style delinquent pleasures while questioning your lacklustre ones. You have him pegged. Now if only you can stop thinking that there's a good chance all of these are mere shadow-truths. And the reality resides somewhere in-between. And in the open smile and the need to connect through unselfconscious, filter-free exchanges. What if he's simply the boy who followed all the instructions, found the loot, and now he's sharing it with you? In the only way he knows.

"You should watch the show. Given that he sleeps like

that, shouldn't be hard to toss in a binge watch every now and then." He says this while looking at the baby, who, come to think of it, does look like he is in a stupor brought on from being heavily and happily drugged.

"Well, your exquisite reasoning might fail because there's also a six-year-old in the mix who doesn't sleep like this . . . or ever, actually."

"Another one at home? Wow, you're brave!"

What do you even say to this? When having a family is viewed and equated to some dangerous act of daredevilry. Feeling less like a mother and more like a high-action stunt double, I know it makes no sense to put forth anything in an attempt to change his view. I don't have to. The conversation is on autopilot.

"Always amused that Indians think children are their greatest assets, when in fact, they are guaranteed to generate low, possibly nil, ROI."

The only thought in my head is: can we locate his reset button and restore him to factory settings?

"So your husband, what does he do?"

"I can't tell you . . . well, I can, but then I'd have to drop arsenic in your champagne."

He smiles. "Oh, you're married to Pablo Escobar."

"He grows the Cannabis trees, I save them." My response cracks him up in several staggered bursts. A loud laugh. A chuckle. Followed by an amused smile as he shakes his head. Like he isn't ever going to get over the fact that the *tree-hugger* can get back at him by poking fun at herself.

In the brief moments of silence that follow, I am

reminded of the precarious balance of things: how we are never more than a moment, a sentence, sometimes just a word away from becoming completely different people. Once they leave our lips, words seem to chart their course along invisible cartographic pathways, carrying us to different places. And sometimes to entirely unexpected destinations from where we may, quite possibly, never return.

"So what's your view on rings—like engagement rings, wedding rings?"

Am I missing a big global trend here? People are expected to have a view on politics, movies, plays, books, countries . . . This somehow feels absurd and intimate, as if I am being asked which side of the bed I like to sleep on after having sex.

"Keep it simple?"

"Yeah, thought so," he says, looking pointedly at my simple gold band.

"Am guessing you're thinking more like Tiffany's five-carat yellow diamond?"

He shrugs, like that can actually be on the cards. "Five maybe inconvenient to lug around, so perhaps three, maybe four . . . Hey, does your wedding band have anything on it?"

His level of just-get-out-there-and-say-it is backed up by this confidence that we are somehow girlfriends who've stuck it out from kindergarten to high school, sharing intimate details on everything from morning ablutions to first crushes.

"Yep," I say, hoping to close the matter with a non-rude yet telegraphic response.

"Can I ask what it is or is it too personal?"

I slip off the gold band from my left ring finger and hand it to him.

In retrospect, it seems like a frightfully peculiar thing to do. All I know is at the time, it was an earnest attempt to add a much-needed air of casual by-the-wayness to this line of conversation, which had somehow meandered into the intensely personal.

He reads the inscription on the inside: Let's make the stars sigh. Looking surprisingly solemn, he hands the ring back to me. "And have you?"

Best way to answer a question like this is with a question. "So when do you pop the big question?"

"Yeah, about that. Not sure. We're both not in a hurry. We love what we do. She's——"

"A Victoria's Secret model?" How in heaven's name did that slip out? I am genuinely mortified now—I feel I need to rap my own knuckles. No amount of explaining can explain I really am not this kind of person. Politeness is my uncontested métier. I have written the manual on kindness and civility. I see boundaries where other people see empty fields and rush in. This is so completely and shockingly out of character. Also, criminally stereotyping. But he hasn't even noticed!

"She could be. Only Nat's a hedge fund manager," he says with a smile that he had to have borrowed from a strutting animated character who practices it in front of the mirror.

"Oh, perfect," I manage to muster up some default politeness.

"Is anything?"

It has to be rhetorical. Or maybe it isn't. Because rhetorical will imply he's introspecting. All evidence points to the fact that introspection will be time wasted for Tom Ford-meets-Tiffany.

"So my dad must have thought he'd grow old with my mother, I mean don't they all? But one fine day she just leaves him. And he marries this totally crazy woman. Like white coats-asylum crazy. I think she couldn't wait for me to leave home or preferably die, whatever came faster."

I've always felt obeisance-level awe for those engaged in mental health healing—psychiatrists, clinical psychologists, even school counsellors. I mean, how do they not implode from the weight of receiving prickly, and in most cases, dismayingly personal confessions? I also feel an urgent need for full disclosure. I want to blurt out to Seat 7A (let's just call him that for now) that I am entirely ill-equipped to respond to this nugget of family dysfunctionality. Even if I manage to channel Deepak Chopra and Paulo Coelho with a sprinkling of Gibran, I am certain I'll fall abysmally short in my response. What are my options here? Nod understandingly like I too have a bitch stepmother? I don't. Pretend I understand the pain of being abandoned by a mother? I don't. Or simply flip the emergency hatch and make my way out? I can't. He is still looking at me. With earnest eyes? How dare he! How dare Beckham-from-Wall Street look at me like my six-year-old does when a toy he thinks will float like a ship in his bathtub, just sinks.

"Well, look how you turned out." No. No. No! It is

exactly the kind of lame, banal, hollow remark that shallow people (who aren't really listening to you) are wont to make. It covers a broad spectrum of responses—you've done okay, you are all right, look how you overcame your adverse circumstances, you are nothing short of a winner—when really what it means is I have no damn clue what to say to someone like you.

In his place I'd have burned me a neutering look so intense it would have ensured me speechless for the remaining duration of the flight. He simply raises a single eyebrow and follows it up with a grin. "So you're saying people must get messed up early in life to do well later?"

I can't thank baby enough for his impeccable timing: he opens his eyes, smiles, and gives me the look that says, 'You have two minutes to get that feed ready before I morph from photo-worthy cherub to toxic banshee from hell.' It is a relief to focus on pretending to perform brain surgery—opening up a carton of formula, pulling out a sterilized bottle, putting it together—concentrating hard on something I know I can do with my eyes shut. Only so I can use my actual focus to find a suitable response.

"I mean look at it this way. Too much cossetting could have turned you into a tree-hugger. What good would that be?"

It isn't the best second serve. Certainly isn't the stuff that scales the rafters on empathy or wit. But at least it brings on a big smile devoid of irony. From both of us.

It is the exact moment I sense a truce. Also the exact moment I feel the subtle shedding of the metal-enforced armour I have been wearing for the last twelve hours. Breathing easier, the conversations continue despite the never converging points of view. Unplugged, unfiltered, unceasing.

The landing protocol kicks in. And Seat 7A returns from the toilet in his suit, looking all set to clang the New York Stock Exchange opening bell. He settles into his seat, spa fresh and smelling expensive clean.

"So can I invite you and your husband for a drink?" he asks.

I smile a thanks-but-no-thanks smile.

He gets it but chooses to act like he doesn't. "Come on, I've got to meet Escobar . . . at a bar?"

I think even my toddler rolled his eyes.

The plane lands with a gentle thud. He is still waiting for an answer.

"You know what, this is insane. You can't spend fifteen hours talking to someone and never meet again."

I shrug. "We're just two people on a flight, we don't even know each other's names."

He nods. "Right! Okay, let's start from the beginning. Hi, I'm—"

"No!" I cut in like I am announcing an emergency landing. "You know what, let's not."

He stares at me for a minute, refrains from asking me why. But clearly he is undeterred. "Okay, phone number?" People around us are leaving the aircraft.

"How about this. It's Wednesday today. Let's meet next Wednesday for a coffee? You can tell me in detail how people like me are out to destroy the world and I'll tell you why you should stop trying so hard to save it."

I have gathered all my things, including my semi-awake livestock, but oddly enough, I am still glued to my seat.

"So there's this place on Fullton Street. Attilio. Six tables, small, tiny. Best food. Unbeatable coffee. Once you have an Attilio espresso, you'll kill yourself before having any other coffee. Next Wednesday?"

Now the economy passengers are walking past us. We are the only business class ones still seated. "Somehow, I always took you for a decaf, no-foam, non-fat, soy latte type," I say. Perfect. Hide behind more meaningless banter.

"I can be old school. So Attilio's then, next Wednesday, 3-ish?"

I try reminding him I am not a coffee drinker. But that conversation goes into another silly loop, faithfully following the trajectory of all our previous conversations and stilting so off-topic that what was actually being said was somehow lost. My boy is telling us to get a move on. After monk-like patience for fifteen hours, he is finally showing us who he is: a little person who can squirm and stretch himself so taut that he can be mistaken for a hardwood octopus.

"I need to go," I say, making paltry, busy movements but remaining firmly in lockdown mode.

He puts out his hand. "Hang on, I might need some good counselling on why I shouldn't invest in an overpriced blood diamond for my fiancé's three- or maybe four-carat ring."

"So will you go first or should I?"

"Why can't we go together? Introduce me to Escobar."

"Please carry on. You probably don't have too many bags."

"Just the one here. I'll be out of the airport in a minute. But why leave like strangers?"

For some reason I am still in physical *and* verbal lockdown mode. He is still waiting for an answer. I don't have a logical one. Like most of my recent actions and puzzling inactions, this is led by instinct. For the record, I hate my instincts. They throw logic under the bus and make me feel and see things light years ahead of when the rest of me is equipped to make sense of them. After all the banter and the laughter and the cringing and the teasing and the criticizing and the confessing, I have seen it. A small red flag, valiantly fluttering in the distance, demanding to be seen, heard, and honoured.

"What are you doing here? This is odd—shouldn't we exchange numbers? What's your point?" He throws me a sentence strung together by question marks and genuine bewilderment.

I am standing now, trying to move in my spot, while the economy passengers are shuffling past us with turf-protective watchfulness. He's still trying. "Wait. Are you feeling guilty about something? Because you always feel guilty . . . or is this your way of being good? But what's not good about this?"

I know he is looking at me. I finally look up at him. "Because if nobody wants to do what's right, what's good, then what's the point? If you can't be illogically good, uncomfortably good . . . what's the point?" If he is surprised by my disproportionate reaction, I am dumbfounded. Was this just lofty blathering brought on by dangerous levels of fatigue?

The shuffling and filing out on both aisles around us continue without disruption. I can't quite place the look on his face. Is he trying to decide if I have played back some filched Obama lines with the help of an invisible teleprompter or has he somehow heard what I was really saying, without even knowing it myself? Understanding what I hadn't said or even fully understood. Finally, he lifts a downward fist and opens it with dramatic panache.

"Mic drop," he says and shrugs like he's conceding defeat. "There's no competing with that. So I'm just going to borrow from that crazy dude with that crazy smile—Seat 7B, you make me want to be a better man."

I am trying to think if he meant Jack Nicholson. But mostly I am just thinking that eight hours ago I'd have defaulted to two possible reactions, full-bodied cringing or an intense eye roll. Somehow, the only thing I feel now is not something you should feel for someone you've met while being transported from point A to B less than twenty-four hours ago: a sense of complete knowingness that I am going to miss this moment when it's gone.

He turns and pulls out his overhead bag and is about to cut into the now dwindling line of economy passengers when he looks at us—my squirmy baby first and then me.

"I have a feeling there's more stuff I'm going to need to tell you. Lines from movies, shit that makes no sense and shit that does . . . Phone number? Limited to emergency texts only?"

"Love covert ops, but I'm afraid I don't use burner phones." That's me creating walls with mindless repartee.

"Come on, I meant your number for emergencies."

Perfectly reasonable ask. Also, it felt right. So right that it had to be wrong.

"911?" I say, trying to be funny while knowing it is miles away from funny, reasonable, or even civil. It is, if anything, my shield against a force more powerful than gravity pulling me in a direction I don't fathom and am terrified of being sucked into.

He nods, steps into the aisle, and in a few swift, long strides disappears from the aircraft, without looking back.

Weathering a Wednesday Storm

As an energy trader, you get weirdly cool at stuff that totally redefines multitasking. Like learning to speak for hours without taking your eyes off the bank of computer screens in front of you; hammering furiously on the keyboard while answering multiple questions and talking into a phone—"Hey Jay, check the stockpiles!"—making sure you take anecdotal evidence like who just sold his big-ass SUV so you can join the dots to the possibly related fact that crude oil prices are going to drop before Christmas. All the while seeing the graph in your head that says OPEC has seen its price basket of twelve crude oils decline by thirty per cent since October . . . Turkey's moving troops to the border . . . Invasion in the offing? Buy! Sell! Boom!

But when you pull off your headphones and finally spit out that stress-mauled, juice-sucked gum from your mouth, you know the only thing that matters in the day is this— you hit the trade on the sweet spot, when it was hotter than a bull on fire. The CEO walks past you and taps your shoulder. Make no mistake, that's a testosterone-packed fist bump saying, "Dude, you made a fat killing today. It's all clocking up." To that year-end seven-figure bonus is what is left unsaid but heard loud and clear.

Our go-to bar is The Whiskey Room. The vibe is always high octane. Good day, bad day, you're all calling it a day in the only way a man should. Actually, that part might be debateable. Some of the guys are going to get higher than the Empire State. It's not my thing. Not that I don't do it or haven't done it. I don't need to do it. Natasha just messaged to say she's at a client dinner. So if I want I can just continue with the guys here. Only, I prefer to end the day with a long run and a movie. A movie on my eighty-inch high-definition television is my guilty pleasure. My bad. Too many guilty pleasures to nail it on just one. But movies are my meth. My crack cocaine.

I have absolutely no plans to stop at Attilio's, but somehow I do. Old man Attilio is surprised to see me in running gear. He's so used to seeing me dressed for work, while I dash in and grab a coffee to go. He knows I am not here for dinner. Actually, I'm not sure why I am here either.

The old man gets behind his coffee bar, reaches instinctively for a tea cloth, and starts to wipe down a small espresso cup. I shake my head, letting him know I'm not having coffee right now. He's puzzled. "Dinner, then?" he asks in an accent thicker than his mother's traditional home-style pasta sauce. I shake my head. "Um . . . just wondering if a friend of mine came by . . . I had recommended your coffee . . . so . . ."

This sounds so pathetically lame even to me, it has to sound like I am drunk to him. "Okay, okay, your friend, huh? He is coming here when? Dinner tonight?"

I shake my head and try to explain. "No, not dinner. I told her about your coffee and I think she may have come sometime during the day. Three-ish?" The old man is processing this.

"What she look like?"

"Uh-um . . . She's medium height . . . dark hair . . . brownish, reaches her shoulders. You may not notice her until she smiles. She's got a big smile and it comes very, very suddenly. And when she listens to you, she looks at you . . . only at you, and her head tilts to one side."

Attilio looks at me for a few moments, then shakes his head. "No. No. She did not come. But I think that is good description. Very good. I will know when I see her."

He's watching me like he's trying to figure out if I need to be escorted home. I'm so freaked out by our weirdish exchange I think I might actually take up the offer if he makes it. "I better finish my run . . . Ciao, Attilio." And I'm out of there.

Okay, so that just happened. No. Idea. How. But, make no mistake, I am not smitten by a stranger. Not my thing. Certainly not this particular stranger. A woman so steeped in domesticity, not a looker (made zero first impression on me), and who has this way of making you think you might just be wasting your life. Because somehow you're shallow. And somehow she's saving the world. What the fuck's up with people who need to serve up guilt to feel good about themselves?

So why did I come here? I told her about this place. What can I say, I'm old school—I show up. In case, just in case, she'd changed her mind and showed up to experience what real coffee—flavour, body, aroma, acidity, sweetness, and aftertaste—should be.

That's it. Done now. Moving on.

Wednesday School Meetings

I have the best crew at work—representation from Bulgaria, Chile, England, Colombia, Germany, India, and of course, America—a regular mini UN rogues' gallery. Everyone believes they are changing the world, even if we've been unsuccessful in changing our hyper-cramped loft offices. Everyone's overcommitted and underpaid. Which is probably why we all have distinct dual (triple in some cases) personalities and job descriptions.

José, who can tell you the global bear population statistics faster than you can say Baloo, is also our resident Shokunin on Japanese food and all things fashion, and a questionably successful blogger on the same.

Axel Brandt is German but didn't get the national memo on efficiency—his desk is a minefield of papers and used food containers so old, he can start an exotic epidemic at will.

But, he's a fierce climate warrior by day, jazz pianist by night, and has a tendency to deliver unfunny one-liners in a growly laryngeal voice.

Our boss lady and my dear friend is Abigail Mendoza. Ask for a quick show of hands for who knows her real name and you might be shocked to discover hardly anyone. She is universally referred to as Max. Just so we're clear, it's Max, as in Mad Max. A moniker earned for her propensity to breathe fire and rage against stupid people. Stupid people being the ones who show a lack of empathy towards race, gender, colour, climate change, animal rights, maybe even parallel parking! It's simple: she just equates selfish people with the head lice of civilization. If I'm making her sound like the activist from hell, it's probably true. But she's also a woman who can make you laugh till you choke, and fight for you like you're her two-day-old cub. Funny and a penchant for misplaced loyalty, what's not to love?

"Did you bring me some more diamonds?" She's beaming at me with pleasure and anticipation. The diamonds in question aren't mined in Johannesburg or sourced from Antwerp. They come from a career *halwai* called Haldiram. He'd be pleased to know his *kaju ki barfi* is equated with the most aspirational stones in the world.

I can see the rather substantial box I had dropped off at her place last week has travelled to work. "*These* diamonds are a girl's best friend," she declares with four pieces in her mouth. José waits to be offered some, but there is no sign of that happening today. He sighs and turns to me to find out if I enjoyed my India trip or the week at home after that more. Without waiting for a response he starts reeling off details of the meeting we have to attend.

"No! Not that arrogant Excel sheet masquerading as a man!" says Max between mouthfuls of diamonds.

"Well, he's the CFO and he's going to sign off on the orangutan film funding we are hoping to get. So we might consider sucking it up and treating Mr Bean Counter like Mr Brad Pitt for now," José says, mostly to Max.

"Oh, I met one of those," I tell them. They both turn to look at me.

"A bean counter? Or Brad Pitt?" José wants to know.

"Well, strictly speaking, not a bean counter. More like a Wall Street type . . . Not Brad Pitt, no. But chiselled-ish . . . Overly self-aware. Get this, he has a tattoo that says 'What's the point of fuck you money if you can't say fuck you?'"

They are both a bit stumped. Then José goes, "*Billions!*" Like he's just won them in a game and not mentioned the name of the show. Max pops another diamond into her mouth and shrugs. "So not Nelson Mandela, then?"

"Not quite," I tell her.

"You met Brad Mandela . . . where exactly? India?" asks Max.

"Technically, mid-air. He helped me get Azad's diaper changed."

"Whoa!" they both go in perfect unison.

"Yeah, long story. I have to take off for a couple of hours—Wednesday school meeting."

"Want my hip flask?" Max offers helpfully. She's actually waving one at me.

I smile at her. "God knows I'll need it. I mean the big question plaguing me through these meetings is always this: how can I possibly be this inadequate?"

José looks at me, puzzled. "What? Harmless school moms do that to you?"

"They are an army, José! An army of all-knowing Mother Superiors and all-achieving Tiger Moms, with a sprinkling of omnipresent Helicopter Moms, who, when they speak, make me realize I've already doomed my six-year-old to a fate of changing tires in a small-town auto workshop. Only because he hasn't started Kumon classes, computer coding, *and* swimming with a certified coach."

José takes that in, then breaks into a smile that suggests he's going to be turning water into wine. "Tell them he's already enrolled in exotic male dancing classes. Do you know what those guys make per hour?" Told you, José can always be relied upon for unusual, mostly un-useful facts.

"Ditch the bitches." No prizes for guessing that's Max's deep, meaningful advice.

"No, I just can't. Seems wrong. I like to volunteer for class activities and field trips, only because I know it makes Azaan really happy."

Half an hour later I'm sitting in the midst of a class meeting that begs the question: why does Azaan's happiness matter—at all?! With all the strife in the world, you'd imagine the school moms would cut each other some slack. But no. There's the non-working mother silently judging the full-time career mother (who has very little time, even to be judged, really), and then there's me, the not-so-glorious in-between. 'Ah, so you work but you can take off any time?' So you can't be too important. And because you're probably all over the place, you can't be relied upon to bring all the attendant benefits that were meant to augur well not only for your child but also to the life of the school. 'Did you say you also have a toddler at home? You have a part-time nanny to attend to him while you work with other kids, teaching them the importance of saving the planet?' Subtext: is that even a job? Further subtext: is that even a life?

Feeling like an imposter whose child might actually resort to the only profession he's showing any predilection towards—dog walking—I head back to the office. Mind you, not in a 'big-ass SUV', which Seat 7A suggested I had to be using to ferry my brood.

It started with him telling me he was about to go in for a pat-on-the-back gift to himself: a limited edition Bentley convertible.

"See, the thing is you imagine a Bentley to be all about old-world British refinement, but then with this bumped-up power convertible it's like—yeah, it's all that, but I am going to make it a fun toy for the wind to sweep through my hair," he says.

I have no idea this much psychobabble goes into the choosing of an automobile.

He turns to me. "And you? Let me guess, big-ass SUV with two baby seats?"

This is humiliating not because of his assumptions of my predictably lacklustre life in comparison to what he poses as his irrefutably exciting one. It's upsetting to be boxed in. I hate it. Hate being the victim of what someone decides to believe is precedent.

"Oh wait, you're a nature type. So it can't be a gas guzzler. . . . Prius?"

See what I mean? So, he was right. But who takes pride in boxing people like they were made of (recycled) brown cardboard?

Don't know about the Bentleys, am just surprised they haven't, as yet, discontinued production of those who drive them and unhesitatingly slot the rest of us into convenient boxes.

Another Winning Wednesday

Closed trades early today. So I start my day at 0430 hours. In the office by 0600 hours. Reading, soaking, gauging, mentally prowling. Then, wham! Trading time at 0700 hours. Hope to make a killing by 1400 hours. All en pointe so far. Fab fuckin' day already. By rights I should be checking my wardrobe choices for the weekend at Raoul's Winery. Lots of toned bodies and wearers of cashmere, relaxed and set for al fresco lunch amongst the grapes and the grapevine—does it get better? Actually it can. If Natasha can make it, it will clock a ten. Unfortunately, she's in Paris for the week, stuck in client meetings. But see, that's what I love about Nat. She's so damn focussed it doesn't get any sexier. She knows what she wants and she'll cut through the clutter and get to it. No waffling. No sentimentality. No confusion.

Even as a freshman at Northwestern, she knew exactly where she was headed: the world of high finance, minus any predictable obligatory detours like building homes in Cambodia or volunteering with Planned Parenthood.

I remember the day we met three years ago. She'd come into the juice bar after her yoga session; I had just come in from the gym. There she was. Moulded perfectly in her sexy workout gear, sipping her juice, and talking on her phone—a glistening goddess—knocked me dead. I'm not sure when Sheryl Sandberg started leaning in, but I'll bet Natasha started when I was learning to play with Lego bricks. Cool thing is you never rescue someone like her. She's happy to invite the first punch like a pro boxer, telling her adversary, 'I'm tougher than you can imagine. Let's do this.'

She loves her job. And I love mine. Three weeks into seeing each other told me everything I needed to know: we were a match made in hard-working, high-living heaven. Don't get me wrong, she's not some hardnosed bitch (okay, at times she can be—and that's a good thing) who wants to be CEO at thirty-five (she wouldn't mind that at all) and never have kids, dogs, and a big warm fire. But not just yet. We'll know when we're good to go. Meanwhile, a rock the size of Africa for an engagement ring can't hurt, can it?

And despite what Seat 7B might say, there's *nothing* to be gained from being subtle and understated. Well, to be fair, she doesn't actually say it, she looks at you like this is somehow beneath her, or that I am selling out. In this case, buying out. And it's not just about the ring. Like the time we were talking about headstones. Not in a macabre, contemplating death way. More like how-grand-is-your-life way.

So I ask her what will the words on her headstone be. She doesn't even think for half a second and goes, "She cared."

I'm like, really? That's so generic lame, so everyday.

She asks me what will mine read. I don't have the exact words, but say, "More on the lines of 'He Danced'. Maybe even get specific and put in brackets Katy Perry."

She doesn't look impressed as I hoped she might. Instead, she looks confused. "The Smurf-coloured hair?"

I smile because it feels like I have just cashed in all my winning chips in Vegas. "No, she'd moved on to a very sexy platinum by then."

She's still looking confused. "Hmmm."

Not the reaction I am expecting. It's time to put humility aside. Hell, it's time to bring out the big guns.

"So there was this insane party thrown by our brokers two years ago," I tell her. "Insane. Bartenders from Ibiza, David Guetta doing the music, celebrities from everywhere. And guess what, I got to dance, very briefly, with Katy Perry."

Seat 7B just keeps on looking at me—clearly, she isn't getting how classy this shit is.

"He danced . . . as in I celebrated life and adding Katy Perry just tells you the scale. Right?"

She stares at me for a really long time and goes, "Right." Then smiles like I'm stuck in second grade.

She doesn't actually laugh, say something screwy, look impressed or look unimpressed, and yet it feels like such a thorough put-down. You know what this reminds me of? Remember Ari Gold in *Entourage*? Foulmouthed, loveable power player and legendary movie agent? When he gets mad at someone he says, 'Shoot yourself in the head with a large calibre bullet.' I feel like I have just followed his orders. So what do I do? Act like the infant she obviously thinks I am.

"What does 'She Cared' mean, anyway?" She has to stop looking at me like she's speaking to a very small child who may not understand what she's about to say if she doesn't say it very s-l-o-w-l-y.

"Cared . . . as in she loved . . . she was empathetic."

Again, said like I am incapable of comprehending this noble (totally sarcastic here) idea. "Empathetic? You do realize what's buried inside empathetic?"

She obviously doesn't. So I clarify. "Pathetic."

I think she's been upended here. And yet she just tilts her head to one side and looks at me with a very amused smile, like it's all confirmed in her head now, and she's officially hooking me up with her six-year-old for a play date.

No Sushi Wednesday

José's post-presentation rules have to have been shaped by Napoleon Bonaparte's—or was it Winston Churchill's? (not that it really matters)—philosophy on champagne: in victory you deserve it, in defeat you need it.

Max, José, and I are heading back after a three-hour session at a prestigious private school in Queens. Our pitch went off brilliantly well: animated, excited students, a supremely energized buzz around internships, and an unprecedented number of student sign-ups as volunteers through the year. Heart-warming and on plan. Until the head of counselling implied having this 'handy tag' on their CVs could prove useful for the high school students in their forthcoming college applications. He reduced our passion and mission to a useful little CV line for college applications, or so an incendiary Max thought. She invoked her inner cheetah, bit off his head, masticated his brains within minutes, and walked away from what might best be described as the carcass of the man. All things considered, it was still a superbly successful meeting.

"Let's celebrate with lunch at Haru Sushi, three blocks down. Better than a Michelin star gig, cheaper than a deli."

Yep, that's José. It's a given that if José wants to go there, then the place will, at some point, find its way into becoming a pop culture phenomenon. And if by chance it doesn't, you can be sure José himself will start to blog about it, aggressively, just to prove a point to us at the office. In his books, the fact that I'm not clapping my hands in anticipation makes me an ingrate or a philistine, most likely both. He takes his eyes off the road to frown at me. "Don't look that way, it's sustainably sourced salmon. I checked!"

"Oh, it's not that at all. Just that I can't get this picture out of my head after something this guy on the flight said."

This gets Max's eyes off her device. "Brad Mandela? How much shit did he say?"

"I mean it was a fifteen-hour-thirty-minute-long flight," I say in my defence. Or perhaps in his.

José takes his eyes off the road to exchange a look with Max. I know that look—united by simultaneous eye-rolling. Max simply says, "Yeah, and the last time I spoke to a passenger on a flight for fifteen hours straight, Mastodons were still roaming the earth."

Minus any prompting or logic, José informs us, "Mastodons are any species of the extinct mammutid proboscideans in the genus *Mammut*, distantly related to elephants."

Are they implying there's an elephant in the room? Before I can figure that out, José, sounding dangerously cranky-hungry, demands to know, "Am I turning in for Haru Sushi or not?"

I need to tell them why I'm being squeamish. It's entirely Seat 7A's fault. If only he hadn't turned around and asked me, "So what do you evangelize?"

I remember thinking, oh great, so now he's suddenly Steve Jobs. I ponder for a moment and say, "It would be alien to you." Might have shut anybody else up. In his case, I'm almost certain he gets a charge out of being underestimated/challenged/argued with and whatever else it takes to tell someone we are never likely to be on the same page so let's not try.

"Try me," he says and pulls out his phone and taps open an app that allows him to use his fingers to draw. "Go ahead, write it, draw it, say it—it can be a word, a sentence, a shape—I'll get it."

I use my finger to draw this:

"Less equals more?"

His expression seems to suggest this is so excruciatingly underwhelming I should be disqualified from his game.

"Get this, I evangelize the exact opposite! More is so much more fun," he unburdens his divine revelation for my benefit.

"Yes, I'd imagine if you didn't equate success with excess it would feel like death by a thousand cuts." It feels like I am constantly speaking under the influence of a polygraph test. Unfiltered truths just pour out with the specific intention of rapping this grown man on his well-manicured knuckles.

"And you probably think everyone on Wall Street who lives well is morally bankrupt." He's still grinning, still so thoroughly pleased with himself. "But it's got to be more. Less doesn't get you into a Beyoncé concert, tickets to the Super Bowl, a house in the Hamptons, or entry into those private dining clubs where sushi is eaten off the naked bodies of hypnotically beautiful women." He seems so deeply hypnotized by his materialistic euphoria he is on a non-stop nonsensical roll. "I love that I have a very expensive toilet that warms up and fires a very powerful stream of water up my . . . you know. Cost a couple of thousand dollars and I love that I didn't think twice before getting it installed." With that the Pope of Conspicuous Consumption wraps up his enlightening sermon.

Do I really want to ask him to address the ethics of buying a commode that costs thousands of dollars more than it needs to? I honestly have no idea where to start responding to this genre of evangelizing. So I do the next best thing: get into the minutiae of the meaningless. "Well, the sushi description certainly clears up one thing, there is always an argument for Brazilian waxing, no matter what."

This just cracks him up like he is going to choke and I will need to tell the stewardess to abandon the eighty-year-old and resuscitate my neighbour instead. "You know some of them are Brazilian waxed, some just let it all hang out."

As far as I am concerned, this becomes, by far, the most disturbing thing he'd utter through the course of the flight. I sit there feeling grossly inarticulate, while swatting a rush of awful, awful images from my head. I can tell he is basking in my discomfort.

"Well, there's no accounting for taste."

Just when I think it can't get worse, he emphasizes the last word in a manner that I know is going to be seared into my brain and haunt me forever.

Wednesday
at the Hamptons

There is something to be said for driving with the roof down to the Hamptons. If you have the classiest woman in all of New York State on the seat next to you, undaunted by the winter air, her hair in a scarf, oversized dark glasses, even Audrey Hepburn can fade to black. Yes, Natasha is back from Paris.

Our CEO, Larry Goodman, is having his annual party, an event so audaciously no-fucks-to-give high-end, I'm willing to bet it can make even Seat 7B relinquish her rigid save-the-world principles for a day. Maybe even forever. Get this, twenty thousand square feet of interior space sitting on six acres of beach-facing land. Larry's mansion stretches into a two-tiered infinity pool, has a tennis court, home theatre, fitness room, and ten bedrooms. It can give the president of any country a case of real estate envy. There's more: George Soros's mansion is just a five-minute Ferrari ride away. George effing Soros, legendary hedge fund tycoon himself!

In another fifteen minutes we'll be mingling with the who's who of the finance world and with a lot of celebrities who just happen to be Larry's neighbours and friends. Jimmy Fallon—a neighbour and a friend. I can be standing next to Fallon, sipping a Long Island Iced Tea, discussing last night's guest on his show. Did I mention that on the spectacularly endless ice-topped bar, hyper talented bartenders will be pulling off old-world cocktails at one end, while at the other end an ace molecular mixologist will be serving contemporary cocktails with ingredients so eclectic that a sensory overload is guaranteed? See, more is more, Seat 7B! More is how the winner takes everything and throws a party that totally slays it. Everything else that you propagate is a zero-sum game.

Hey 7B, do you remember the conversation about the one thing that makes a Sunday brunch perfect? It was a rapid-fire question to be answered simultaneously without thinking, without hesitating. And this is how it went down:

"Mimosas!"

"Jalebis!"

"Really? Jalebis? Do you try to be super-ordinary or does it come naturally?"

Genuine question, wasn't being rude. Of course, you followed it up with the sort of explanation that makes no sense to anyone but you.

"Other than exploding with crunch and sweetness and

fun, it's like tasting home. It tastes like Sunday. It tastes like how life should be."

Whatever. "Home is waking up on a Sunday and being ten minutes away from perfectly done eggs Benedict and mimosas made with dry Prosecco with just the perfect splash of freshly squeezed orange juice. Ten minutes away is a crucial ingredient in the mix—I can't emphasize that enough. I don't care if I have to splurge several thousands extra on rent. Remember, the smartest real estate tycoon in history said it best: location, location, location."

Your response to that was more unexpected, more condescending, outrageous, and hilarious than I ever imagined someone like you to be.

"You're jerking yourself off? Enjoy."

"I can't believe you just said that. Diaper bag armed, death over impropriety, be-socially-conscious-or-die-guilty mommy, did you just say that?"

You looked me in the face and said, "Don't judge people by what you think you see. Big movie guy, remember the most anti-social person created the world's greatest social network."

"Whoa! Throwing sass like confetti."

I may not have told you then, but I did concede that round to you.

Big Drama Wednesday

I haven't got a full grasp on the point of after-school activities for six-year-olds. Why can't they just come home and play, instead of 'learning' to play? I know their days of babyhood cuteness must give way to middle childhood learning. Yes, I got the memo—disguised as a link—(while drowning in ten thousand others from school on a weekly basis, masquerading as fun reading for mommy and daddy) preaching that the brain has pretty much reached its adult size and it is to be the phase of great cognitive creativity and ambition, making tens of billions of synaptic connections.

But here's my question for the synaptic geniuses, how is a child who slips tentatively into a Tai Chi class, only because he's mortally frightened of Little League baseball, feeding those synaptic connections? System error? No answer? Thought so. Caught on the back foot, you say maybe drama will do it for him. So here I am: skidding in, just in time for drama practice before next week's big Christmas performance. I'm 'volunteering' (what that means is I am a human glowstick for the rest of the mommies to see; the same ones who show up for everything, every day). I nod-smile politely as I make my way past the various huddles of mommies, props, kids, more mommies, and three earnest daddies.

As for the play in question, someone on the drama committee decided it was time to give six-year-olds a reality check—so why not focus on the most dismal part of the zeitgeist. Cue fanfare music: presenting a Christmas play that sucks the pleasure out of being a carefree child because it shows you Santa's helpers can get laid off but they must learn to find meaning and joy (and of course alternative employment) along the way.

Since I lack the requisite zealousness to go bounding forth and becoming a part of the PTA, I shall hold my peace and cheer my son, while I struggle to make myself useful in my volunteered position of props assistant. I share this daunting responsibility with Nancy Kellaway, whose son is playing Santa Claus, the same one who shall sack the minions, one of whom is Azaan. Nancy is always so exactingly turned out, I get a sense she has a personal shopper, spa, and a full-service hair salon factory-fitted in her Porsche Cayenne SUV. She also has this addictive need to dispense helpful parenting advice every second she speaks. So, in the unlikely event that you're not daunted by her red carpet-ready aura, you really ought to dig a hole, climb in, sit there, watch, and learn.

My son's monumental dramatics career at this point involves being dressed in a red suit—since he is playing an office drone—and being tossed off Santa's team and the stage within five minutes of the play. But as the great thespians and Azaan's dad will tell you, it's not the size of the role that matters. "Who knows, maybe he'll pull off a De Niroesque you-talking-to-me method actor move, right after he gets the sack from Santa, and live on in the hearts and minds of fans forever." Yep, that's the dad.

Meanwhile, Nancy wants to know what activities I've started Azad on. Gentle reminder: Azad is fourteen months old. I'm holding a wand from the props box and I wonder if it will be faster to whack Nancy on the head and knock her out cold or try to cast a spell and turn her into a Banana Republic shift dress-wearing toad. I'm too slow to execute either option, so she just carries on enlightening me.

"Have you given Einstein Cubby a go?"

Have *you* thought about how sadly oxymoronic that name is? Have you thought about the fact that it was Einstein himself who said, 'The only thing that interferes with my learning is my education'? Those snappy lines are, of course, only coursing through my head while her lines are live and sharp.

"They introduce Schubert and Mozart at an early age, scientifically done to enhance both left- and right-brained activities. Tell me, what sort of music do you play for him at home?"

For God's sake he's barely done with being an embryo and between the ten balls I have up in the air on a daily basis,

I don't think I care if he listens to Daft Punk or Korean Pop. "I have a wonderful young Indian nanny. She loves doing her work to Bollywood music. Azad's a regular little head banger now."

She squints at me like I am the ant that everyone stamps on and nobody ever manages to see. The squint speaks a full sentence: your son's future career, *regardless of what he chooses*, is doomed.

As I help a little fairy into her ballet shoes, I am reminded of Seat 7A's infantile comment about careers.

"But how is making kids aware of the environment a career?"

"How is trading in oil not being short-sighted, supremely selfish, and disturbingly indifferent to climate change?"

It's like I've spoken to a wall, because the guy next to me is just smiling and waiting to ambush me with more nonsense.

"Oil equals money. And no matter what anyone says, money gives you the best home court advantage."

I'm about to tell him what I think of this, but he raises his hand like he's the only boy with the right answer in the classroom.

"Do you know what Harvey Specter says?"

I brace myself for the ridiculous.

"Caring only makes you weak. Just wake up, kick ass, repeat."

I must have looked really stupid because he starts to deconstruct his fridge-magnet speak for me. "Harvey? Harvey Specter? Harvey has everything on the cool guy checklist. Lawyer, name partner, best wheels money can buy, swag like you can't buy, and most important, he doesn't take shit." He's desperate for me to understand the enormity of quoting a slick TV character. "*Suits!*"

"Ah. The plural of you." I think I am saying it in my head, but apparently it is delivered to him in person.

Celeb-Spangled Wednesday

Right now, Natasha and I have just entered this celebrity-spangled event. Natasha's client, who deserves to be name-dropped but can't, all because this is his wife's charity fundraiser and she wants no loose tongues or smartphone-wielding paparazzi—absolutely nothing that can launch a debate about the excessive nature of the event. Can't say I blame her. The paps and the naysayers always seem to have a hard time deciding if these folks are crusaders or vultures. Suffice it to say we are on a boat, but it could pass off as a galaxy that just happened to land and park on the river. Lit up by more than fifty thousand LED lights, waiters—looking like moonlighting movie stars—weave through guests with appetizers by a Japanese Michelin star chef, the guests are wrapped around a three-sixty-degree bar counter, and at the centre of it all is an Olympic pool-size dance floor. It's exactly what puts people in the mood to dig deep into their pockets and write that cheque to change the world. It's also what puts them on a high. Often, an unnatural one.

In a most outrageously sexy all-black bathroom, I notice three lines of pure white powder contrasting dramatically against the glossy black counter. As I turn to leave, two young boys stumble out of a stall. Blonde and fine-boned, they could be Justin Bieber's untattooed twins. I realize now who the stash belongs to. I also realize that one of them is the hosts' son. It's the perfect time to make a discreet exit.

Natasha, nursing a glass of champagne, chats with her client, the host—relaxed and easy. I can never stop being a fanboy each time I see how she holds her own with anyone anywhere. Some Cirque du Soleil style performers are taking over the dance floor. I feel like I've just been sucked into Baz Luhrman's *Great Gatsby* party scene. This isn't just dazzling, it's monumental, and something that I am certain Seat 7B would call 'a spectacle of prodigal waste'.

She uses terms like these all the time. It usually begins with totally obscure questions that have no relevance in real life. Like if you had to leave this planet and could carry only three memories with you, what would they be? Then there was this one: "Complete the sentence, I was born to . . .?"

No brainer for me. "I was born to live big."

She thinks for a long time and then says, "Yep, I can see that. I, on the other hand, was born to do small things . . . with big feeling, maybe."

That's the equivalent of settling. That's staying stuck in

your comfort zone. That's a total cop-out. "That's what you were born to do? Really?"

"Yeah, I like the size of my world—it works for me. It might seem unbearably small to some, but it's got everything inside it that makes sense. Well, on most days, that is."

"So you don't want to . . . to say, join the UN or be in a position to influence people to do more of this environment stuff that you do?"

She shakes her head like she's feeling surer by the minute. "Working with young people, watching them discover how they can help preserve the planet by doing little things is big enough for me . . . yeah."

A life made up of playing small, I seriously don't get it.

"You don't get it, do you?" She smiles at me like she's just read my mind. "Let's see . . . so, socializing for you probably means being at the best party at the best address in town. To me, that sounds like a death sentence. Unless I know it's a place where you can be yourself—exactly who you are, honest, happy, tentative, funny, vulnerable, stupid, sad, and through it all, know that there's a chance of forging a real connection with someone."

After that cliché-filled monologue, she is quiet for about thirty seconds, then she chuckles. "Also, the other party . . . way above my pay grade."

Natasha and I move to the dance floor.

Just to conclude, I was born to live big. And no, that wasn't a party you were describing, Seat 7B; this is a party.

Perfect Wednesday

A Max rant is in full swing. I hear dispatches of sarcasm and irritation flying at sound altering speed from her room all the way to the lobby where I've just entered. I pass Axel who tells me, "It's *wunderbar* she speaks her mind to that ill-informed sponsor." José looks like the anxious parent who has no control over his child who's taken to biting other kids in the playground. He turns to me. "They're funding the shoot in Indonesia, it's okay if they ask some dumb questions." I smile sympathetically at him and head into Max's room.

"I'm afraid the orangutans don't have proper videoconferencing facilities, neither do we have any evidence that they are telepathic. So, very little chance of me telling you how long it's going to take to spot them and film them. Three days or three months, your guess is as good as mine. Let's talk to the agency today. Okay?" Max bangs down her iPhone with such vigour I feel certain that every Apple employee at Cupertino can feel the vibrations.

José has entered the room and hovers nervously next to me. "So are we going to have to look for alternative sponsors?"

There's an array of nerves in the vicinity, some jangling and others overwrought, all in need of calming. "They have deep pockets, they are committed to our cause. Okay, so they asked some stupid questions, but frankly, at such short notice we don't really have much of a choice, do we?" I say in the hope of being the voice of reason.

José nods in emphatic bobblehead manner, while Max, who has temporarily ceased breathing fire, looks from me to José then settles on me. "Excuse me, who loves to say you always have a choice? Wait, it's you! But then you have the perfect man, the perfect kids, the perfect dog, the perfect nanny, the perfect exhaust fan, the perfect underwear, perfect window panes, even the perfect mother-in-law—so you've never had to make a choice, right?"

Don't mistake that for an attack, it's pure unadulterated love, just badly expressed.

"Perfect nanny? Also, not sure about the kid, well, the older kid. He just finished telling me he never wants to go back to school and wants to become a full-time dog walker. Oh, and he wants to give up his latest after-school activity, Tai-Chi, because it was supposed to be meditation in motion, but the way it's practiced in school, everyone thinks it's about beating each other up."

"Did he actually say meditation in motion? Those words?" José asks in awe.

"I think his dad told him that and now it's a parrot thing."

"Get him out of school. Let him walk dogs! He's way too smart for school," says Max. "Also, still perfect, you're gonna have to try much harder."

Max has known me for seven years and she almost has legal rights to sound proprietary about my supposedly perfect life. Or poke fun at it. Or get mock weary of it. She also knows I do nothing to perpetuate this myth. But who gave Seat 7A the right to systematically poke holes in my life condition like he was an ace White House correspondent and I a nervous, fact-withholding press secretary?

"Are you using your blankie?" I ask, because the cabin is freezing and Azad is wrapped in my blanket.

Looking thoroughly amused, he hands me his blanket. "You can have my *blankie*."

That's when I realize I used the kiddie short form.

"You know, after having kids, some words are never the same again."

He loves this. "Like sex?"

I shoot him a look, like this is seriously inappropriate. "No. Like blanket forever becomes blankie. Horse is horsie for the foreseeable future. And I suppose I'm going to stop saying boo-boo to a cut once he's sixteen. But for now, it is what it is."

"And you're telling me through this . . . this daily

drudgery, you're still making the stars sigh and you have the perfect love and the perfect life?"

Okay, first of all, it's really hard to tell if this man thinks I am his mentor or simply his dartboard. The grin on his face implies it's most likely the latter. Let's get some shooting practice and some laughs at her expense. I'm about to give him a talk on boundaries but instead, with zilch warning, I become the bisected biology project, the splayed frog, who somehow puts itself together and starts explaining what you did wrong.

"Perfect love? First, let's get this out of the way: that's an oxymoron. Love, even if it did come to us with a user manual, we'd remain ill-equipped to follow its instructions— even if they were Ikea-easy. It's supposed to work like a song? Damn those songs because love just splutters and stops in the middle of the day when you're discussing who will step in for the nanny. The nanny who is absent more than she's present and who tends to make the most hideous wardrobe and music choices. They say love is romantic. But here's what else it is. Some days love is too big and too hard to handle, on some love is also unbearably small. Love is magnanimous on some days and on others love just hides and can't be found. It can be naggy. It can be tired. It can be liberating and still be claustrophobic. It can be a crabby pre-schooler. But it can also be sublime. Yes, to answer your question, it can make the stars sigh. Mostly, when you least expect it to. Like when you've stayed up till four in the morning finishing a story that has to go into print, and you can't, for the love of God or your child, get out of bed at four fifteen when he's crying because he had another bad dream. So the man next to you gets up, bumps loudly into everything in his path, and gently picks up the child. He doesn't look like George Clooney when he's doing this. He's wearing a severely oversized T-shirt and shorts he should have thrown away three years ago. He's wearing sliders with socks, which you hate. But he's carrying that child with such love and chooses to blast Adele's 'Skyfall' because he thinks it will make the child go back to sleep. Of course, neither the child nor I can sleep. Adele! I love her, but her dispatches of culpability and her high notes at that hour? But yes, I'd say that is one of the times love seems perfect. Invincible even."

He looks like he's in dire need of the Heimlich manoeuvre. It strikes me then that everyone in our cabin is asleep, except for us. Even the crew has been spookily invisible for some time now. Not at all comforting when you imagine fancy GQ boy might be having a life-threatening physical reaction to my diatribe. Although, come to think of it, he's looking at me like I'm the one in need of help. Like I'm the one who needs to be medicated.

It really doesn't matter one way or another, because this is what he gets out of my honest, heartfelt rambling of intensely personal feelings: "So, Adele, you like her?" I nod, more out of not knowing what else to do than from genuine engagement with the question. He's smirking now. "Adele. What the hell do people do at her concerts? Try to hit the high notes with tears streaming down their faces while they send texts to their exes?"

Despite myself, and everything I think he's not, I burst out laughing. He looks so pleased, like he's singularly responsible for splitting the atom and recoding the genome.

Wednesday Per Se

atasha loves Per Se. Not because it's Thomas Keller's acclaimed New York interpretation of The French Laundry (although she does think anything with a French accent is civilized). Not because it has spectacular views of Central Park (of no consequence during her frequent client dinners here). Not because they offer an exquisite nine-course tasting menu so delicate and fine it feels criminal to eat it and not frame it (anyway, Natasha hardly eats, either she's too wired up or cleansing). Not because it's her favourite chef's second three-Michelin-starred property (wait, that may have a role to play—class is Natasha's resting pulse). Mostly, I think it's because she looks and feels at home in places like this. It's been weeks of frenetic work and transatlantic travel for her. She's been back in New York for a week and finally things at work are a little more even keel. So I booked us a table tonight. Just us. No friends. No colleagues. No clients. A good old-fashioned just-us date night.

The sommelier makes her an impassioned speech about the Renato Ratti Barolo. She nods like a queen and a bottle appears at our table. She's barely had a few sips when her phone starts buzzing. She looks up at me. "I'm sorry babe, I have to take this." Then glances at the message, types urgently, and hits send. Puts her phone face down on the table and smiles at me like nothing happened, or is likely too. But I can tell she's disappearing a little already. "Something urgent? Thought you guys were more relaxed this week?" I ask.

She shrugs. "Ditto." There's a searing economy to how Natasha never over explains, never tries to make a big deal, never feels compelled to go on and on about the choices she makes.

Nat is a pro at work. She doesn't believe in bringing it home or asking for opinions. She doesn't need your opinion. I love how secure she is. She's on top of it. No matter what it might be. "So this is a new fund, a new pitch?" I ask only because she's more preoccupied than she should be on her break. "Not new. Unexpected. Peter's stepped back from the French fund, so I've been asked to take the lead on it." Wow. That's big. She's a masterclass in downplaying the big. That's Nat. Nothing's too big. "That's fantastic! Reason to celebrate. Let's get something more than the Barolo!"

She smiles distractedly, her phone buzzes again. She glances at me, then flips her phone over, takes a look at the message, and turns it face down again. "Yeah, good news and maybe, not such good news."

"How can heading the fund be bad news?"

"Basically, it means spending at least three weeks a month in Paris for the next couple of months."

Oh fuck. Bummer. No, it's a good kind of bummer. Natasha is a star. Not only that, she comes from a family of stars. Her dad's a legit banking guru. Celebrated alumnus of the legendary IIMs in India, he stepped into the hallowed portals of a foreign investment bank and never looked back or down—probably spent more time moving in high altitudes than the Wright brothers themselves. Along the way he married his super sophisticated college sweetheart and moved to the United States. Two years after they moved, Natasha was born. Of course, Natasha knew exactly who she was going to be even before she was born. If your dad was invited to be a member of President Barack Obama's Advisory Committee for Trade Policy and Negotiations, I'm willing to bet, you'd be as badass about your career goals as Nat is.

Now, I may not be blue blood banking and financial services like she is or a blood relative of big money, but I am a heart relative. So I totally get that not seeing her for three weeks in a month is simply collateral damage.

"You okay, babe?" she wants to know.

"Yeah, of course. I think this is great for you, for your CV, and it's only for a few months. But this is big league. Let's do this." She leans over and kisses me. Her phone starts buzzing again. She ignores it.

Our first course comes in. Looks like an exhibit from the MOMA. Pure art. Natasha's phone rings, yet again. She mimes an apology and indicates she's stepping out for a moment. Of course I'm okay. If you're going to play at the big boys' table, you're going to have to put yourself out there and go for it, hell for leather. You grab opportunities wherever they may be. Paris or Poughkeepsie. As my good friend Harvey Specter says, 'Ever loved someone so much, you would do anything for them? Well, make that someone yourself and do whatever it takes.' This *is* what it takes.

When I said this to Seat 7B, she just didn't get it. I mean I'm not surprised. She operates from a different planet, yet remains firmly deluded that she's in the know of everything. Everything! She actually told me, "I'm a noticer; sometimes I wish I didn't notice so much." How is she unable to nail a straightforward answer to a simple question? Ever? I asked her a simple question: "So how come you made this trip without one kid?" and this is what she said, "Oh, I was in Delhi for barely a week—a family wedding. I'd love to have brought the older one, but my mom-in-law was visiting and he is the love of her life. I couldn't take him away."

I didn't get it then, I still don't. "Did you want to take him with you?"

"Well, I'd like to have. Ideally. But she was going to be with us for just two weeks—she'd have to do without him for a week—I just couldn't do it."

"I don't get it. I'm sure your son didn't get it." This woman doesn't get it!

"I think he may have, and if he didn't, I'm hoping he

will at some point, and when he's older and it comes to someone he loves, I hope he finds it easy to say, I got this one, for you."

"So you think teaching him to constantly step back is a good thing?"

She shrugs.

"Here's the thing, if you want to get somewhere, you don't take your eye off the ball and that means putting yourself first. Golden rule: put yourself first."

She looks at me and smiles. "Golden rule: put those you love first."

"So you're going to teach him to wear his heart on his sleeve and forget about having goals, forget about getting somewhere?"

"Why can't he do both?"

"We don't live in Disneyland. Like a shark, you have to keep moving forward or you die."

"Why does everything have to be so rabidly single-minded?"

"Because those you call rabidly single-minded get ahead—Usain Bolt the shit out of their lives and get ahead of everyone else."

"What's the point of getting to the finish line first when everyone who matters has been left behind?"

This woman needs to course correct, needs to go to reality boot camp. Only, she looks much too comfortable sitting cross-legged on her seat with her kid asleep on her lap. Much too comfortable. No course correction in the offing, for sure. In fact, she looks all set to ask me yet another disconnected-from-reality question. "What's the one thing you should never have to do?"

"Lose." There is no other answer to that question. Unless you're her, then there has to be an unlikely, unreal, impractical, useless take on every no-brainer question. "And you?"

"You should never have to tell someone how to love you."

I give up.

Natasha's back, she sips her wine and looks at me, "Looks like I have to head back to Paris tomorrow." And I need to get a restraining order against Seat 7B getting within ten feet of my head.

Natasha puts her hand over mine. "Hey, you okay?"

"How can I not be, you're crushing it, babe!"

Prospect Park on a Wednesday

It's the wonderful sound of early morning no-sound. I'm adding the finishing touches to a presentation we're making to the NYC Department of Education this afternoon. I embellish generously with quotes from Henry Beston, naturalist and writer extraordinaire. I'm beaming at the screen, marvelling at the beauty of how it's all come together, and that despite its pedantic limitations, on some days PowerPoint can wake up and sing like an Italian soprano in her prime.

I spot Azaan's just-woken tousled head behind my laptop.

"Hi buddy, you're up early."

Uh-oh, he's wearing that expression only a cello can play.

"I don't want to stay for Tai Chi."

It's only been three classes and I am told my role here is to persist. Not give in. Control the narrative. I try to channel Amy Chua's iconic and unrelenting Tiger Mom and think of how when her daughter Lulu lags at piano practice sessions, Chua drags her doll's house to the car and tells her she'll donate it to the Salvation Army if she doesn't have an incredibly difficult piano piece by a French composer mastered by the next day.

Azaan climbs into my lap and keeps looking up at me like only I can save him from being decapitated. It doesn't help that he has big brown eyes—which he has to be time-sharing with a spaniel—and when he blinks his eyelashes literally rest on his cheeks. "Okay, how about we decide we're going to miss today's class . . . then can we talk about it?"

Do not judge me. I did put up a fight. Let's just say I believe in choosing my battles.

He shakes his head. I can see voluptuous tears balancing precariously at the rim of his eyes, poised to pop out in the tradition of the best weeping animated characters. This is going to escalate. And here it comes: "No Tai Chi. Never. Never!" he announces through a quivering lower lip.

"Okay. Do you want to tell me why?"

"I hate it. Andrew punches!"

Obviously, the Tai Chi teacher has been overthrown by a six-year-old tyrant, my son's arch nemesis since Pre-K. Admittedly, Azaan is gentle. Too gentle? But since when is it okay for little punching tyrants to call the shots? Literally! We've got to take this up with the school.

"Is there any other after-school activity you'd like to try instead?" Still trying to control the narrative here. I intend to win the war. Didn't General Patton say battle is an orgy of disorder? Why bother with silly battles then?

He nods. See, this is a good thing. He knows his mind. Take that, Amy Chua!

"Dog walking." Okay, maybe don't take that just yet, Ms Chua.

"Sure you can do that, but can we talk about school activities first?"

Just as I'm about to go into an elaborate explanation of how many wonderful things he can do in school, three things happen to ambush my chipper, winning-the-war pitch.

My phone beeps madly with a tsunami of texts.

Azad cries to announce the bear has woken and is likely in desperate need of a diaper change.

Azaan cries even louder: "I don't wanna go to school today!"

Where's Riz when I need him? I almost forgot he's on the red-eye to San Francisco for a meeting. Perfect timing. The messages are from my nanny. A series of one, maximum two, word bursts: Mother sick. Doctor. Now. Finish. Come home. Drop. Reach late. 12 can.

Eight text messages to tell me she'll reach at noon. While I appreciate the telegraphic detailing, today I'd have appreciated her timely presence so much more. I am presenting to the governor of New York schools, woman!

The previously mentioned no-sound morning accompanied by the rhythm of a perfectly unfolding day comes to a grinding halt. Azaan is having a quiet meltdown and begging to go to the park, while his brother is waddling around the living room—a diaper on banshee duty.

An hour later we're sitting in the park, Azad happy in his stroller and Azaan bundled like an Eskimo, bragging that he knows the names of each and every pigeon that flaps fearlessly close to us. I figure if we get home by noon and Nanny does stick to her '12 can' commitment, I can be well in time for my three pm presentation. A dear friend and co-suffering school mommy insists on calling me Panda Mom (which is the answer to the question: what is the opposite of Tiger Mom?). I've vehemently denied ownership of the sobriquet up until now. Something tells me after today's performance, I might be invited to a royal coronation where I'm anointed and the title and crown shall be mine forever. Immovable. Stuck firmly with gorilla glue and loss of authority.

It's fine. I am just going to go out and say it: I feel like the earth will go into holding pattern if I am not around when my boy looks cello-faced. There. Shoot me. From both sides— glass ceiling shatterers and effortlessly efficient stay-at-home mommies. I can live with it. Happily (on most days).

However, what I can't live with is ambling around in arctic temperatures, wondering if the pigeon called Billywig is on Prozac. Otherwise no creature, big or small, can look this prancingly happy on the brink of what feels like a blizzard coming through. Azaan leads us to the Cocoa Bar and ten minutes later we're warming our hands around mugs of deliciously rich hot chocolate. Azaan's mug has more marshmallows than hot chocolate. But who cares!

As far as I'm concerned, world order has been restored. Everyone's warm and happy—just taking in the magic of a hot beverage on a topsy-turvy cold day.

Not quite the same as when Seat 7A decided to give me his take on the magic of a hot beverage. He was dying for a cup of coffee, but he refused to settle for airplane coffee. Naturally, he felt like he needed to explain his hipster affectation to me.

"Look, there are only two kinds of coffee that a coffee lover should consume. Attilio's espresso. And at home it's got to be from the Chemex coffee maker—the retro pour-over machine used by Obama himself."

I feel like he's waiting for a drumroll before he can finish his sentence. I put on my best Oprah listening pose.

"The White House ordered one hundred and fifty pieces etched with the Presidential Seal."

Oprah won't do. I think he's waiting for me to fold over in supplication—acknowledge his extreme coolness—contort in the galley, if necessary. The infomercial continues.

"Do you know the glass beaker design is so sleek, so iconic, it's in the permanent collection at MOMA?"

He speaks with such reverence, I know now this is not a mere coffee machine. It's a religious cult that extends unwavering support and holistic healing for those with First World problems.

I am ingratiating myself before the universe—I need answers. Why do kids have to lead checklisted childhoods to be considered normal? And why do grown men feel they need to supersize their expensive obsessions to feel normal?

Out of Whack
Wednesday

No telling when shit can go down. Take Jason, he was having a turbo-charged purple patch, a dream run, hitting one out of the park every day for a month. Today, not so much. Now he's trying to ride on his hot streak. Hoping it will go the way it's been going. But we all know hope is not a strategy. He knows this better than anyone. He's a good guy. He's my bro. We started at the same time—everything at the same time. He's ballsy. Knows how to balance risks while maximizing returns. This could be a one-off bad day. Bad day from hell, actually. He's down so much, Larry's smoking from the ears. Jason got the I'm-closing-your-book look from him. Worst feeling in the world when your CEO threatens to shut you out. I've seen it a million times. Guy makes a trade. Blows up in his face. He thinks he can chase his losses, so he puts more money into the trade—goes batshit crazy. Loses all his money.

Jason takes the afternoon off, he needs it—it's been a perfect shitstorm. I take a few minutes off to run down to A's to pick up a coffee. Attilio tells me, "Your friend, the listening friend, I don't think she come." I want to tell him she doesn't really drink coffee.

Of course, one has to employ a high degree of subterfuge to figure that out. So I try telling her all about the mandatory moves to enjoy a good coffee. Attilio's espresso, and then the blazingly awesome Chemex coffee maker I have at home. She listens to me for the longest time. Like really listens. I know I've hit a home run. She's impressed. Finally something I say seems to have gotten through to her. She looks breathless and like she's actually tasted what I'm talking about. "Oh yeah. Coffee. It's a feeling . . . a word you can taste. It's like an Aretha Franklin song. It's like an empire of romance. It's the best of rain and the beauty of snow. Inhale and you can be transported to a person, a place, a song."

Whoa! Way intense! I'm a coffee guy, but even I have no idea what I should say to that. Then she tells me, "There's this Turkish saying about coffee, it sums it up better than anything else: coffee should be black as hell, strong as death, and sweet as love."

The woman is going all poetic genius over my drink. My drink! I have to say what I say next. "Look, I'm going to send you the Chemex pour-over. Consider it an early Christmas gift. Give me your address."

She shakes her head. "No, no, I don't drink coffee."

At first I think she's taking the mickey. She has got to be kidding.

"You . . . don't drink coffee? Really?"

"Uh-huh."

This is just messed up. It's like watching Beckham in that famous underwear ad and asking, 'Does Beckham like to get inked?' No, she cannot be serious. "You feel all that intense stuff about coffee . . . but you don't drink coffee?"

She shakes her head, looks at my bewildered face, and laughs. By the way, she snorts when she laughs. "I mean I've always loved the feeling. Not the drink. It's okay, right?"

I just don't get this woman. And then she says what has to be the most conclusive endorsement of her craziness. "I'll tell you what I do love, though. A good old-fashioned masala chai."

There you go. Nothing, absolutely nothing, can be done to lift her out of her default setting of ordinary.

Vermont Wednesday

We are returning from the Green Team Youth Conference in Barre, Vermont. Not sure why I agreed to José's grand plan of taking the scenic route (seven hours driving time added to forty-eight hours of away-from-home time) instead of the train. Don't get me wrong, I loved the why, what, and when of being there. But the time between the somethings (home and work) and the nothings (needless travel) stretches interminably long. The sticky notes in my head break into a flash mob parading all the things I didn't do, should do, and didn't even know I wanted to do. Like cancel Azaan's after-school Tai Chi class. Sign him up for Astronomy Club. Send out those messages for Riz's family reunion lunch. Have a serious chat with staccato message-sending nanny about her erratic timings. Maybe, I'll skip the last one for now. Azaan and Azad love her. I'm just going to have to learn to love her bad grammar and haphazard attendance.

The Youth Conference is a chance for kids, grades seven to twelve, to learn more about climate change, renewable energy, and how to make a difference in their school and community. I'm still marvelling at the eighth grader who spoke with freedom fighter zeal about the staggering number of initiatives she's working on as head of her after-school Green Club. She was so leaderly she deserved to be called POTUS, in advance. Max was ready to file adoption papers on the spot and bring her home tonight, in the hope that she may run our organization from tomorrow. This is Max we're talking about. Small recap: the same one who, despite her unshakeable commitment to our cause to find and forge an early love for the environment, is also known for her scathing comments about the very people we're hoping to teach, inspire, and convert. Last week, she met a small group of interning high schoolers dressed (and I use the word very loosely) in baggy, oversized objects trying to pass off as garments. Their heads uniformly adorned with headphones large enough to launch them into outer space, wearing expressions that seemed to suggest they had strayed much too far from their mother ship. Max took one look at the boys, turned to me, and muttered, "I do feel for mothers of teens; I also understand exactly why some animals eat their young." I tried to remind her one of them might be the next Carl Sagan.

Is it a coincidence or part of a larger let's-get-a-rise-out-of-her conspiracy that I am surrounded with people who make parenting and kid jokes part of their daily de-stress routine? Even complete strangers, sometimes. Like Seat 7A. He rattled a bottle of Aspirin and went, "Good advice can come to you from anywhere. Look at this . . ." and held up the bottle. "Take two and keep away from children."

Someone euthanize me. I absolutely cannot swallow another movie line, TV show character's ideals, gym poster slogans, or recycled-to-death kid jokes from this man.

"So I take it the big mansion in the Hamptons you want to buy is to be filled with extras from the *Wolf of Wall Street* set, and not children, dogs, or any sort of family?"

"Not a big fan of families. Neither my own nor my uncle's—which I was passed onto like a hand-me-down pair of shorts—have done anything to inspire warm fuzzy feelings towards this miracle called family." He finishes with air quotes around the word he's at loggerheads with: family. Throwing me yet again into an unwelcome conundrum: to smart alec or not.

Imagine each time Mohammed Ali, between floating like a butterfly and stinging like a bee, is poised to land that knockout punch, his opponent yells: 'Hang on!' All because he feels compelled to remind him of his backstory—that his childhood wasn't picture-perfect, that his rubber duckies didn't float in a row. Exactly. That's how hopelessly disadvantaged I feel every time GQ man references his family. I feel like I need to pull my punches, give him a lick-your-wounds timeout. Curtail my joyful exuberance about perforating holes in his cardboard persona. Which, frankly, at the rate we've been going, ought to have more holes than a Braille sheet of music. I do not want to feel guilty. And certainly not about a stranger who called me out on feeling generically guilty.

"It's not just the house in the Hamptons. By next year, I'm hoping to put a down payment for this fantastic one by the ocean on the West Coast. I already know who's going to design it." See what I mean? This is what I get for giving him a graceful timeout. He just scrambles back into the ring and lands a sly uppercut my way. Well, if the rules of engagement are going to be so dodgy then the gloves are off.

"Wonder if people who take on mortgages for multi-million dollar ocean-facing homes are aware of the fact that eight million tonnes of plastic are dumped into that very ocean each year."

"Nice! Doomsday alert on my dreams."

Incarcerate me for wanting my children to live in a world where they can take for granted the clean air, lush forests, healthy oceans, and polar bears who are not on starvation diet plans. And for hoping they don't ever need to wear masks to school like dystopian characters from movies that never end well. But nobody, absolutely nobody, can accuse me of having a Nostradamic bone in my body. I remain optimistic to the point of seeming harebrained. Mawkish. Heedless even. But nothing that resides in the same zip code as doomsdayer.

"So, in your view the way forward is giving up worldly pleasures and living like a monk?"

"Not at all. Although curtailing a little tawdry excess may not be a bad idea. For the world in general."

"Oh, I have zero problems with excess. Thanks to my need for excess I'm here and not carrying other peoples' bags in my uncle's little motel back in Canada."

"So it's either manic material consumption with a total disregard for consequences or a mindless life of physical labour?"

He throws up his hands like this is not even an argument. "But if it makes me happy—"

"You do realize that after a point the joy from acquiring is fleeting at best?"

"My Porsche maybe fleeting past the world, but make no mistake, it still brings me great joy. Every frickin day."

"Not to be preachy, but we're in the worst crisis of pathological consumption that's totally screwing the planet, a world-consuming epidemic of collective madness. Thanks to advertising and the media, we think it's normal, we need it! Honestly, do you really think more Porsches and more homes and more toys you don't need, will help you find more joy? How much incremental happiness are you hoping to find exactly?"

"I'll find out when I get there." He tosses me a cheeky smile.

"Okay," I offer a deliberately innocuous response—an honest attempt to put an end to this unendable argument.

"And by the way, you keep talking about saving the planet for our grandchildren, but if we just commit to not having any, we could solve the problem already."

It's way past dinner by the time I enter the house. It's a school night and nobody is in bed. I hear laughter from the family room. Riz is a dream daddy; just never ask him to get the kids to bed at bedtime. Or feed them dinner at dinner time. Or bathe them when they should be bathed instead of inserting them into an extravagant bubble bath in the middle of the afternoon when they should be napping.

I can see them now. Azad is covered in peanut butter—someone had to have dunked him in a giant Skippy jar and pulled him out just before he drowned—and rolling on the rug. Groucho (the dog, not the husband) is licking as much peanut butter off him as he can, while remarkably keeping pace with the rolling. Azaan is holding his breath while Riz counts down "3 . . . 2 . . . 1!" and on cue Azaan burps. They fist-bump like they've scored the final goal and won the Super Bowl title. All three look up at me—chorus boys in perfect unison. Groucho is industriously licking Azad's fingers clean.

"Mama! Daddy taught me how to burp when I want!"

Riz looks at me with the pride I imagine Stephen Hawking might have felt after he'd discovered a prodigy to follow in his footsteps.

"Really, Daddy?" I'm looking at Riz.

"See, it's a major life skill. Azaan didn't want to go for Tai Chi because Andrew bothers him. Now, if Andrew dares to come near him, he can just burp eight times in a row right in his face!"

How can you not love this man? This completely messed up crew?

Wednesday in Paris

'We'll always have Paris' is one of my favourite movie lines. Yeah, I know, I don't seem like that guy. How can I? It sounds like such disposable fluff. Besides, the movie came out before my time, before my parents' time! Scratch that. No fucking clue about my parents and their times—good, bad, or underwhelming. But hey, it's Bogart and Bergman and trench coats and planes and Bogart with all sorts of swag who owns a café called Rick's, in Casablanca. What's not to like? I'll tell you what. This whole sacrifice thing that Rick pulls off for his girl—letting her go with the other guy while he stays back in harm's way. And when she goes all sentimental on him, he heroically mumbles those famously over-referenced words. Nah, like I told Seat 7B, I'm not about the sacrifice. He should have hopped on that waiting plane with Ingrid Bergman and her aristocratic cheekbones—left the lame-ass husband behind—and they could have had Paris forever!

I told her (Seat 7B) that sacrifice guarantees only one thing: a spot at the back of the line. But she even found a way to justify coming last. "A freight train is pointless without a caboose—it's where the crew are." Caboose! You know, I actually feel sorry for those boys of hers. Really, what chance do they have with their 'She cared' mommy at the helm?

Okay, back to the Paris plan. Heading there with the ring in my pocket—yeah, that's done. Walked into Tiffany's, excavated a three-point-five-carat Princess Cut hole in my pocket. So worth it! Cannot wait to see the look on Nat's face. Obviously, I'm heading to Paris with a single point agenda: to pull out the plugs. Lasserre, near Les Champs-Elysées and Avenue Montaigne—check. Table under retractable ceiling opening to the stars—check. Famed Lasserre chef to place the ring in his signature dish—check (Well, almost check. He's a snob and I understand some coercion is in order. But if you know anything about me, you'll consider it done).

I'm rushing out of the office to the limo waiting at the curb when I walk right into Jason. Returning from a much-needed non-stressed air and coffee break, I'm guessing. Come to think of it, he's been missing for most of the morning session. That was a long coffee he stepped out for. He high-fives me.

"Bro! You're really doing this!"

"I am."

"Oh man, does she have any idea?"

Why is Jason twitching so much? He's jittery. Tense? "She knows I'm coming. She doesn't know I'm coming armed." I pat my jacket pocket where the little blue box sits snugly.

He moves his arms like he's cheering at a game. I'm not sure he's okay. Actually, I'm pretty sure he's stoned.

"Dude? You okay?"

"Hell yeah!" Okay, he's definitely stoned. He's got exaggerated movements. He looks hyper happy in a depressing kind of way.

"Listen, why don't you take a couple of days off?" I think he really needs to.

"Oh man, no. Got to show Larry! The bastard was kissing my ass when I was on a hot streak, now he's all over me like a rash."

"Just take a few days, let shit cool down."

"Nah, I'm getting into beast mode," he declares with chemically-induced bravado and zones out for just a fraction of a moment. Like he forgot he was supposed to be upbeat and in the conversation. Then he returns with a big smile and a misaimed high-five.

"You, my man, go and make that girl feel like a queen. See you when you're back from gay Pari!" He's almost unhinged chipper. He doesn't look good, but my limo guy signals he's about to get a ticket. I turn back, wondering if I should stay and make sure Jason's okay. He claps his hands, salutes, and literally marches off. Fuck. He's being weird.

Later that evening in Paris, I'm standing on the movie-worthy balcony of Natasha's glorious serviced apartment—

wow. I mean, wow. It's in the heart of the Eighth Arrondissement and the view is what every person who's never been to Paris dreams Paris will be. Only, it's better. Natasha's not back yet. But the doorman had instructions to let me in. I'm ready. The champagne's ready. Both chilling. It's starting to drizzle.

It's half past six, Nat is still not back. No sweat. I've made a booking for an hour later. They'll hold it till eight. Nat's having a bit of an unexpected crisis with a client. She messaged to say: *Home in thirty. Latest.*

Drizzle just turned to mad rain. Fuck. The awning over my head sounds like a battlefield, the soundtrack during the grand climax of *Dunkirk*.

Apocalyptic rain now.

She has this thing for rain. Like nearly everything about her, I don't get this either. She, as in, Seat 7B. We had hit the second patch of bad weather on the flight. She turned to me, looking perfectly calm. "So what does rain remind you of?"

Didn't think. Knee-jerk, top of my head. "Missed schedules?"

"Okay. Anything else?"

"A recent survey said rain, winds, and clouds tend to discourage stock purchases and sunny skies promote institutional buying. Get this, analysts are nine to eighteen per cent less likely to make optimistic forecasts during overcast days—photographic memory helps."

"Wow. It's like listening to a PowerPoint deck turn into a person and spew numbers and facts nobody ever listens to."

In my world, too much rain can precipitate a crisis. I don't expect someone who uses words like 'enoughness' to get that. Really. "What? It's what matters. What would you have said?"

Funny thing, she doesn't even need to think. Not for a second.

"Childhood, bare feet, all the tea in China! Masala tea, tea in *kulhads*, home, blankies, books, no work, hot toast, lots of butter, curled up dog, dappled windows, washed streets, everyone you miss and can't be with."

I, on the other hand, am experiencing the inability to reproduce another word. Only because I am not sure there is a response to something like this. Other than being crippled by the unjustified hype. And she's not done. "Also, I kind of take it personally when people refer to rain as bad weather."

I'm guessing I look at her with the face we reserve for passing drunks. She tries to help me. "You have two options here: a) why didn't I think of that, b) tell me more."

"Is there an option c? For full-grown adults who don't eat rainbows for lunch and ride unicorns to work?"

She laughs. Technically, she's snorting. That, by no means, qualifies as laughing.

"Rain Girl, you really need to grow up."

"Why, because you don't get my idea of luxury since it has nothing to do with Bentleys and overpriced green juices that look like piss and cost fifteen bucks a pop?"

She needs a wake-up call, this flower child from the sixties.

"Rain. Huh? Let me tell you how romantic it is. On my way in to the airport in Delhi today, I got stuck on a road that looked like the highway to hell because of some unseasonal rain. Even worse. My Uber stalls. The idiot who was driving me hopped out, opened the hood of the car, and stuck his face in—lit a match too—sucked on some pipe with his mouth . . . This is Uber we're talking about. Uber in your rain."

"Clearly, he got the job done. You're sitting here."

"Yeah, but that is not the point."

"Actually, it is. He's an uneducated nobody whose only major qualification is his can-do attitude. And nine times out of ten, he gets it done, by whatever means—matchstick or blowing into the hood. That's pretty heroic, don't you think? I mean not in the Tom Cruise suspended-with-a-rope-in-black-spandex kind of way. But he did get the car going in the middle of traffic and he did get you here in time, against all odds. So don't blame him. And definitely don't blame the rain."

It's seven thirty. Nat is stuck. Luckily, not in the rain but in a meeting. She's sent a series of texts, apologizing. She's super bummed out. And she doesn't even know it was meant to be the big day. I'm planning to go for broke tomorrow. Pivot and bring it home; it's what I do. Right now though, I'm standing in the balcony, doing something really odd. I have the awning pushed back and I'm getting drenched, in my two-thousand-dollar cashmere sports jacket. Feeling the rain.

How freaking stupid is that?

Un-Valentine's
Wednesday

"Every single restaurant I've tried booking is unavailable! Has the age demographic of Manhattan suddenly shifted to only under-eighteen, infantile, and choking with raging hormones?"

Max has a close friend from Sweden in town for just the day. The simple act of getting a decent restaurant table on Valentine's Day can turn anyone into . . . well, Mad Max.

"Forget it, restaurants and florists have zero *fikas* to give today." That's our in-house trivia king, José, not really helping by flaunting his knowledge via ill-timed Swedish wordplay.

After waiting—whilst mostly threatening to hang up—for a condescending restaurant hostess to decide if she might deign to spare a table after nine, Max decides to hang up and take charge. "I am sorry, nothing can be worth negotiating these emoji aliens, thinly disguised as humans, with hearts popping out of their eyes. I'm picking up Vera and heading home."

In principle, I'm on the same page as her on the frenzy around this day. In reality, I'm mostly just indifferent and rarely vocal about it. Except, and you guessed right, with Seat 7A. Retrospectively, there's a good chance I may have even come across as a Valentine's Day Nazi.

"How can an intelligent adult not see it for what it is: a commercially-authored large-scale programme to raise sales for overpriced flowers, chocolates, and dinner reservations, all in the name of love?"

Mr Big Spender looks like I've just stomped all over his exposed nerve endings. "How's that different from any other holiday or festival? Why is Christmas or Diwali or Thanksgiving exempt from your judgement?" he wants to know.

"Because they're inclusive. They're about family, and making those who are not family also your family, about showing gratitude . . . not ads and candy companies telling you how to plan your day and how to show your love."

He folds his hands in prayer position and holds them close to his face like he's about to harness his inner *chi*. Then turns to me like a great big bolt of enlightenment has hit home.

"Clearly, you see grocery store shrink-wrapped milk chocolate as your benchmark, so you don't get it. The first year, I sent Nat ten bouquets by Manhattan's leading floral design creative director. One of them was made up of something called Black Baccara roses flown in from Amsterdam on the day."

And once more I have an unforgiveable reaction that slips out without suitable warning, "Goodness, how funerally."

I can't decide if my comment is more outrageous or his puzzled reaction more hilarious. "What? The Black Baccara roses or the ten designer bouquets?"

In my head the word 'Both!' is exploding with mirth and clamouring to make an appearance, but I decide to circuitously move forward. "No, am sure your way of personalizing the day is cool. I just have an issue with anything that makes anyone, especially a young person, feel alienated, like they are a failure because they weren't the recipient of a red rose, a syrupy message, or a teddy bear bigger than a car. It's a kind of tyranny pretending to be a love potion."

He shakes his head. "Wow, you're the Grinch."

I shake my head. "Nope, the Grinch hates Christmas. And I love Christmas. We start celebrating from November."

He could be searching for grace and equanimity. But then he gives up and gives it one last shot. "You've never been surprised on Valentine's Day, so you don't get it."

"That could be true. I don't get it. But I do have a spectacularly funny and very special memory of one Valentine's . . . I woke up to find a small rubber plant by my bedside with a note that read, 'You're killing it, babe.'"

Sepulchral silence. With one non-cookie cutter admission, this sanctimonious vegetarian mom has robbed GQ man of his debating abilities. But then his curiosity helps him recover, and he asks, very slowly, "Your man gave you a rubber plant for Valentine's Day and you found this special?"

I tell him rubber plants and I have a grandiose history. I kill them with love.

Blood Knight
Wednesday

I've just been blown away by me.
Paris wasn't on plan. Natasha had a week
from hell, but what good's a guy if he can't
turn hell into some kind of heaven? Rhetorical
question. Anyone who knows me knows
that's a given. It's the Ethan Hunt principle:
the mission is always accomplished. Calling
it Mission Impossible is my kind of irony.
It's always a done deal! I pulled out the ring,
popped the question. She said yes. All we've
got to do now is work out the when and the
where of wedding plans. Macro done. Micro,
no sweat. Minor detour in work plans, though.
Natasha may have to stay in Paris for another
year. So the three-weeks-a-month-in-Paris-for-
the-next-couple-of-months thing turned into a
no-wiggle-room-for-one-year-at least. I mean,
of course, she has to stay back. She's practically
doing the job of a CEO right now. That's

beyond kickass. We've just got to ride out the distance. Piece of cake for us: what are we making these big bucks for if it isn't to fly to Paris or New York like we'd drive to our nearest Whole Foods?

It was a killer day at work. Lots of bad calls. Stress hanging in the air like stale sweat. But you learn to ignore what's happening around you and perform like a Blood Knight. I'm no gaming nerd. Played once at an offsite. Never got hooked on the game. Got hooked on the Blood Knight credo. War will never be hell to this guy. Fighting is meditation. He's not about morality or the motives. Glory is being in the fight. I'm a Blood Knight during trades. Everything else turns to dust when I'm making those calls. When it's over, I start to feel everything: a combination of brain freeze and a body battered with marathon runner fatigue. So when it's time to go out and unwind—which, for most of my kin usually means drugs, sex, booze-fuelled rock 'n' roll, or a happy mix of all three—I really only want to do one thing: fall into bed with my favourite vice. A movie. Today was a day when pigs get slaughtered (trader-speak for buying a position that's too big and ending with getting swallowed). I came out on top, covered everything, and made some. I deserve to indulge in a guilty pleasure. So it's going to be *Notting Hill*. Again. I think people should own up to the movies that give them pleasure and stop being so intellectual about it. You can call it slushy, saccharine, and predictable. Or, if you're Natasha, you can call it cheesy. But it works for me. Each time I'm flicking channels and it's playing, I stop and watch it, like really get into it. That means it's got something. I like the dinner party scene. Gets me every single time. Something about an A-list movie star coming into a super ordinary guy's house and lighting it up.

My mind taps in on the scorekeeper in my head to a certain conversation about a dinner party. Another conversation fated to land in another infinite loop, like everything with Seat 7B almost always did.

"Your dream dinner guest list—from anywhere, any time?" Most of her questions lack even remote evidence of logic and are so perfectly non sequitur that top of the head rapid-fire answering is the only thing that makes any sense. Why think and waste time with proper reasoning?

"It would have to be the gurus of Wall Street—Henry Paulson of Goldman Sachs, Stanley O'Neal of Merrill Lynch, Jamie Dimon from JPMorgan Chase, maybe some venture cap guys like Peter Thiel and yeah, Beyoncé." She starts laughing. Like really laughing. Not a subtle chuckle. No minor snorting. This is *loud*.

"Okay, you just broke the Richter scale of predictability."

I really don't see how my list is so funny.

"All those money men and Beyoncé—what is this, some frat boy fantasy?"

She has a point. Beyoncé would be the odd one out. "Okay, so I'd swap her with Warren Buffet." She shakes her head, face filled with sympathy like I have a rare chromosomal deficiency. "What? I'd be set for life, clinking glasses with Jamie and Warren." She thinks for a minute, then says, "And this lot, this is your lot to . . . make you feel alive and like you've been touched by magic?" Can she not hear herself? "Duh, I'm in a room with the people who make more money than most of the world put together. I'll be ten Red Bulls alive!"

No, she's not getting away by looking at me like she's trying not to wince with pity. I'm on top of my game. Nobody looks at me like I'm a lost case; least of all some judgemental mommy from the burbs. "So who would you call?" I ask defiantly and she doesn't even have to think.

"We're allowed to get people living and from the past—clearly not a big deal for you. I'd want Einstein, Barack Obama, Audrey Hepburn, Roger Federer, Coco Chanel, Carl Sagan, Walt Disney, Hasan Minhaj, my dad, actually my dad would be first on the list, and then I'd also call—"

I have to cut in. "Why only your dad? I mean if you've got to be stuck with family, it might as well be the whole lot."

She looks at me, but she isn't really looking at me. She is somewhere else. "Dad. Because he'd be the most charming guy in the room. Any room. Anywhere. He'd have to be there. It would be my way of getting him back."

I don't get it. "Get him back from where?" Dumb question, when I think of it now.

"He passed away when I was sixteen."

Don't get me wrong, she's not about to cry or do anything dramatic. She just looks like she's not in this conversation anymore.

"Yeah. Dinner was never the same."

Yeah, maybe I didn't think my list through. Suddenly, it started to feel like a *Forbes'* listicle. Maybe, just maybe, she'd have more fun at her dinner party.

Fuckety Fuck Wednesday

On some school days I am convinced I should use Azaan's college fund to purchase cases of wine in incalculable numbers. And drink it all. In a day.

Thankfully, he's over the dog walking as an after-school activity plus long-term career goal. He now aims to be the Frank Gehry of dollhouses. No, you heard that right. Dollhouses equal Barbie, Bratz, someone called Sofia the First, and maybe—still undecided—certain Disney princesses. What's clear is that Pocahontas will not make the list; Azaan rightly assumes she isn't on the lookout for a bricks-and-mortar architect. Not sure if it's a doll phase or an architecture one. Probably both. I find the doll phase adorable and frankly, didn't think much of it until I saw a raised eyebrow from a member of the righteous parenting brigade. "How lovely, he likes to play with dolls . . . but you know that's a trigger for bullies, right?" I could have given her a handy compendium of lessons on gender-neutrality, non-binary choices, unfettered imagination, and other allied freedoms. Instead, I smiled charmingly and said, "At least I won't be complaining like some of my friends do about their sons' hyped passion for sports and the ruined-with-practice weekends, obnoxious coaches, misplaced macho values."

I'm innately comfortable with the path of least resistance, yet I can't deny the acid joy I felt upon delivering that response. Of course, I am aware that I may have thwarted my son's chances of being accepted in any jock squad for the rest of his life. Sensible deed for the decade done.

Meanwhile, no man is an island, et cetera, and certainly this part-time-almost-full-time-but-not-quite working mommy cannot afford that luxury. So we are on our way to a pre-scheduled, pre-perfectly planned play date with Maya, a sweet, friendly seven-year-old school friend. Her mother is the poster child worth mentioning here: high income bracket, highly educated, stay-at-home professional mommy whose sole job description is to craft her child into a masterpiece and put forth into the world—by feeding her brain with carefully curated stimuli since she entered her womb, and feeding her body only free-range chicken, organic broccoli, heirloom tomatoes, and everything GMO-free. Farmers' markets are her Mecca. Whole Foods is her daily temple. I wish she were my mother.

We pull up at 2.42 pm. Perfect. Three minutes to slay the dragons in Azaan's head, cross the moat, and ring the doorbell. A page from a Ralph Lauren catalogue appears at the door. That is Poster Mommy in pristine white linens. I am tempted to go down on the ground and pay my respects to her audacity—white linen on a play date! Clearly, she's got the heart of a warrior princess and a magician dry-cleaner waiting in the wings. Pleasantries are exchanged. Azaan's allowing Maya to glimpse into his backpack, which I've convinced him is an architect's bag of tools. Pick-up times are discussed. I'm about to start walking back to my car in relief when Poster Mommy drops the B-word.

"I have a lovely snack waiting for you guys! Tofu scramble tostadas and oatmeal broccoli pancakes!" Okay then, she has a full-time nutritionist and celebrity chef in her kitchen, while I just fed my kid non-artisanal bread (cardboard) and Cheetos (poison!) for breakfast.

Like the voice of an angel, Azaan's chorus begins to play forth. "Fuckety-Fuck-Fuckety-Fuck-Fuckety-Fuck-Fuckety-Fuck."

Forget the wine. I'm resorting to opiates.

"Oh, Azaan is weird about broccoli," I offer, sounding more blasé than anyone can possibly feel while imagining myself signing a no-profanities contract if ever my son gets invited to another play date.

I have no idea why, but in this bristlingly awkward moment, where my parenting skills are a stand-in for the bullseye, I have left the perfectly spruced up driveway and transported myself back to my seat on the plane, and am finishing up another unfinished conversation on parenting with Seat 7A.

He is looking at me like I am a three-horned doleful monster. "Four of you actually have to sleep on one bed?"

"Don't have to. End up."

He shakes his head. "So you have beds, but you indulge them, and in some warped way you like to think of it as love or nurturing or some such thing?"

"On nights that they can't sleep alone, one climbs into our bed and the other one is eventually carried in. How can that be a bad thing?"

He puts on his superior child psychologist face. "Look, I have a misguided friend who became a father at twenty-seven and now I see what it's done to him. His four-year-old draws this spastic stick figure, one leg shorter by half than the other, some crazy green hair, and feet like he has a parasitic infection that causes extreme swelling. He calls the picture 'my dada is hero'. Frankly, if I was his dada/daddy/whatever, I'd a) be super insulted, b) worry the kid has zero talent and is, maybe, vision-impaired, c) make sure he never draws again. What does my friend do? Sticks a gold star on that absurdity. Kid thinks he's Van Gogh. I think my friend's just created a career pussy."

Tripping on his own hubris and lack of sensitivity, he smiles like he's standing in an auditorium filled with applauding parents. "A parenting expert and a mind rarer than radium," I say.

He can be thick as a deli sandwich, but at least the sarcasm isn't lost on him. He shrugs and opens out his palms. "Look, the kid is already slated to fail. That's what all this excessive delusional praise and cuddling does. Hey, but if you want to squeeze four people into a queen-sized bed and ruin their self-esteem and your sleep, that's your call."

"Five. Sometimes the dog climbs in too. Three things: a) it's a king-size bed, we upgraded when we realized most nights we'd end up five on a bed, b) there are days when you want to toss them all off and sleep on satin sheets *alone*. I mean, all alone. But then that feeling—those little bodies pressed up against you, smelling of baby shampoo, that gentle breath against your neck—no spa can rejuvenate your body and soul like that feeling does, and c) you may believe you have all the right answers before you have children but once you actually do, you realise parenting is mostly the Zen acceptance that the questions are always going to outweigh the answers."

That night when we were in bed minus the boys and the dog, I tell Riz, "So, I can't, for the life of me, figure out where Azaan's picked up this new cuss mantra that he uses liberally and musically. I feel like—"

Riz cuts in. "Oh! Fuckety-Fuck-Fuckety-Fuck-Fuckety-Fuck!"

I disentangle my head from the crook of his arm. Sit up and stare at him. He looks sheepish but goes for disarming. "In my defence, a fuck slipped out when this guy ran in front of our car. I thought it would be more age-appropriate if I turned it into a fun thing. I did it seamlessly, made it kind of Disneyish . . ."

"Stop, please stop . . ."

Rooftop
Wednesday

By some small miracle and unexpected math, despite a string of bad weeks, we are celebrating quarterly profits in epic style this evening. This time it's a chic new rooftop garden venue on a vertigo-inducing floor—offering a dazzling view of Manhattan's photogenic skyline.

On our shared calendars, Natasha and I had marked this extended weekend as NYC. Earlier in the week, we took stock of the situation and flipped the entry to Paris, knowing the whole time it wouldn't happen. Larry takes his quarterly-profits parties much too seriously for me to skip one for a plane ride to Paris. And Natasha takes her meetings in Paris too seriously to opt for a plane ride to New York.

So even though it's a non-ambiguous plus-one invite, I am minus-one. Which, for a lot of guys around me, is actually the gold class option. I mean, look around, every woman here looks like she just walked off the set of *America's Next Top Model*. If I wasn't an atheist, I'd go so far as to say Wall Street traders are God's cherry-picked angels. Could this whole shebang be anything less than a miracle? The patron saint of hedonistic pleasures has to be sitting in the heavens, smoking a Cohiba Behike cigar and grinning at us with satisfaction.

Is there anyone here who wants to be anywhere else? I'm willing to bet my bonus the answer is a stadium-filling no. Isn't that the only litmus test for how fucking terrific your life is?

Only Jason doesn't look like he'll be nodding in the affirmative to that today. Or hasn't for several weeks now. He's sitting at the bar, high as a kite. It's simple: he's been losing too much. He's edgy. He's stuck in a tunnel right now—no light, no exit sign, no way out. But hey, that's the price you pay for these returns. High stakes, steep falls. I have to talk my buddy out of this loop that could morph without warning into a crash and burn downward spiral. I'm nursing a bacon-smoked Manhattan and am about to walk up to him when I see a blonde goddess trying to light her cigarette but the wind won't let her. I rest my glass and cup my hands around her cigarette and she lights it. Long inhale, longer exhale. This is what sexy looks like in a white barely-there dress. She looks up at me. "This is so unreal cool!" she says. I feel oddly let down by her voice, and even more by her observation. That's what happens when you see too many old movies. You expect a woman who looks like that to sound like Lauren Bacall. Her date, Roger, swoops in, high-fives me—yeah, we guys do that a lot, and not just when we are trading—and whisks her away. She turns back and smiles. Wide smile, perfect teeth. Empty.

I'm looking at the incredible garden we're standing in and wondering who even gets to see this on the ground and here we are on the thirty-seventh floor.

So she—I don't mean the Lauren Bacall-could've-been, but Seat 7B—in yet another random question-out-of-nowhere drill, asked:

"Funny memory? Doesn't have to be crazy, laugh-out-loud, insane funny. Just funny and stuck in your head."

I think. Think hard, actually. But I just can't cough up a crazy funny memory. Not sure I have too many funny memories. I'm a doer. An achiever. I don't do funny or cutesy. I also hate being stumped. So I am working hard, hamster-on-a-wheel hard, to come up with something. College? Sure, there were moments. Some binge drinking thing, but nothing that really jumps out. I want a humdinger. So I buy some time. "You go first."

"We'd just moved to this little walk-up in Brooklyn, our first home together. A friend had given us this spectacular, luscious, huge indoor *Ficus elastica*, a rubber plant. It was the best-looking thing in our home. The friend, who had an incredible green thumb and was passionate about plant care, told me how to care for it—it needs moisture but not so much water that the soil gets soggy, and remember, always wipe the leaves clean, dust build-up can interfere with photosynthesis. Then he let me into his little secret to keep the leaves super glossy—wipe them with a touch, just barely a touch, of Vaseline."

I'm thinking where is this going? The only thing funny so far is how unfunny her story is starting to sound.

"I followed the instructions like they were a sacred, daily religious ritual. My husband had the car and I used to get a ride with a colleague, Rish, who lived one block away. Despite my military-precise plant care routine, every morning I'd wake up to find a perfect leaf had yellowed and mysteriously fallen off. Undaunted, I'd go through the water, wipe, Vaseline, love, care, bless routine. Then, holding the fallen leaf, I'd rush out to meet Rish. I'd drop the leaf in the trashcan and get into his car. He'd put on a mock sympathetic face and go, 'Deepest sympathies for your loss.' It became a daily ritual. One leaf. Every day. Condolences from Rish. After about a month, I get into the car and Rish looks at me with all the mock-sympathy he can muster and asks, 'How many leaves left?' I shake my head and tell him it's the last one. He nods gravely. Then, looking like he's at a funeral, asks me, 'How's Riz holding up?' It cracked me up! It still does." I can tell. She's snorting instead of laughing.

"So you don't have a green thumb. Or, like I said, over-caring can never be a good thing."

She just shakes her head, still smiling. "Or, as my friend with the green thumb said, you're the girl who over waters plants because she doesn't know when to stop giving."

About that. All I can say is, this woman-girl-infant needs to grow up. All her stories have Disney endings.

I still can't remember a funny story. Luckily, we are

already locking horns over giving and giving stupidly, according to me, and of course she is so busy belabouring her point she has completely forgotten it is my turn. Typical.

I should have called her out, asked her how the self-appointed guru to young climate warriors failed to keep a simple houseplant alive. Oh wait, her Valentine's Day story about the rubber plant just made sense. *You are killing it, babe.*

Let's Get Wild
Wednesday

Let's Get Wild is a quarterly event organized by us for school children and their parents. A warm fuzzy event to bring home the dire consequences of big oil and gas companies going nuts drilling through the wilderness. Now, if we say it like it is, most likely we'll be branded alarm-raisers or sleep-inducing tree-huggers by nearly everyone, other than the informed and the believers. Luckily for us, Max is the product of fourteen years spent in the trenches of an industry that can package anything into bite-sized, sparkling, and if done right, entertaining ideas of communication. Advertising.

"Nobody wants to buy a product. They want to buy a story. A feeling! So let's make this feeling so awww, no parent and child leaves without adopting at least one animal and knowing at least one reason why they're doing it."

We set up a giant gazebo in a park and fill it with drop-dead gorgeous pictures of endangered animals. Here's the awww: the kids can, through a wonderful organization, adopt an endangered animal by paying a small annual fee, and wait, they get a glossy picture of the animal and a miniature soft toy replica. That's a triple whammy, or as José loves to say while patting himself on the back, "This is fun(silent d) raising!"

I'm surrounded by a group of kids looking with pure adulation at a gloriously cute picture of the Snowy Owl, as I tell them how we can save him from extinction. "They are white, with some brown spots and have golden eyes. But small ones, not like the huge eyes we normally see on owls."

"Is that Hedwig from *Harry Potter*?" That came from a miniature Hermione Granger aglow with formidable seriousness of purpose and an unwavering stare. You do not mess with that determined little persona. I tell her I believe Hedwig was a Snowy Owl, but a female, hoping against hope that my Potter knowledge serves me right. I quickly move into weaving a story around how these magnificent birds depend on places like Alaska's Arctic National Wildlife Refuge to survive. But big oil companies refuse to stop drilling. And that means . . .

I know this as well as the stories I read to my children—on loop. There are times when Azaan wants the same story read every night for three and a half weeks, which basically amounts to reading without reading. Nobody loves Shel Silverstein more than I do—*The Missing Piece* is a classic, I never tire of its profoundly simple wisdom. I never cease to get a thrill when the Missing Piece, with a wedge waiting to be filled up, rolls along and reshapes himself—essentially, completes himself and learns to roll along with his friend. We've read it twenty-seven times. My love isn't diminishing, but my mind does wander. The question here is: where does your mind wander when it's on autopilot?

I have the conviction of miniature Hermione when I say this: Seat 7A has to have reversed-engineered every single conversation between us to instigate an equal and opposite reaction. Make it contentious, if possible, deliberately perverse, and whatever happens, get that last word in. It isn't surprising then that when my mind idles, it reverts to finishing an argument or a conversation we began that day. And winning it!

"So you actually think you're going to save the world by getting kids to adopt near-extinct animals for $100 a year? Hilarious!"

I am not even going to waste a moment of my time or my brainpower trying to explain this to him. Partly because I believe being deliberately obtuse is one of the frequently employed strategies from his infuriating arsenal of annoyances.

"Just ask us, the guys with the money, and be done with it. Take our donations. Dust your hands, move to the next project."

My head is telling me to practice transcendental meditation or maybe even fake my own death, anything to avoid falling prey to another senseless argument. Nah. My head is too slow—my words have decided to carpe the hell out of this diem.

"Wait. Which cave are your offices in? Did you not know that you are the problem? Big oil is Darth Vader. Come on, Mr Vader, even you know that greed to drill ensures we rob these species from their homes, their lives, and their future."

He nods sagely, like he may actually be getting it, may even feel a smidgen of regret. Then he turns to me, eyes dancing, big smile like he owns the world, and says, "Still makes sense to take our big money and save the world."

"Okay, tell me which part of this you didn't get? Oil drilling, oil selling, oil trading—you create the problem, why would we come to you for funding? Explain that? You are the problem. You don't get to buy your way out."

"Also, this may shatter you, but a lot of the people who could possibly flood you with funding believe this is all over-hyped. Waving a smoking gun without a shot. Just saying."

"Hey, you've been reading what we say, only you didn't read the full sentence. One of the nature types, as you like to call them, said that this isn't a smoking gun; climate is a battalion of intergalactic smoking missiles."

He stretches his legs, pats his still impossibly perfect hair. "Everything has a price. Everything can be bought. Everything."

Witnessing this riveting display of arrogance, I have only one question in my head. Is it incumbent upon me to continue, as a duty to my job, my beliefs, my children's future, to try and explain the very basics of common sense and humanity to this man? Wait, did I say man? I meant wealth-aggregating algorithm.

He continues like a determinedly stuck record. "Everything has a price."

"Doesn't."

"Has worked for me, every single time: tickets, restaurant bookings, getting someone to change their mind, sweeping someone off their feet, tilting the balance in your favour—works every single time."

"Not for everything. Not for everyone. Doesn't."

"Does."

"Doesn't."

We were kindergarteners in the sandbox. Someone was going to toss a handful of sand in the face and someone was going to cry.

"Does too."

"Okay, so does it bring back someone you lose?"

A beat.

Another beat.

No sound.

And then he recovers. "Oh, come on, that's just unfair."

"You bet. Losing someone is always unfair."

She's still here
Wednesday

Natasha flies back to Paris today. We've had the best weekend plus two days. She's still in bed. I'm up. I've taken an off from work since Monday—this waking up early is a curse and a super power. Mostly, it's just an occupational hazard. But it works for me. When I wake up before the world does, I step into the balcony and look down on Manhattan, and I get my first king-of-the-world invigorating rush. No better way to kick-start the day.

I don't need that today. When you make love to a woman like Natasha, you wake up with a cache of feel-good chemicals coursing through your brain. The effects of which are so far-reaching that the best nutritionists, trainers, life coaches, and therapists working in tandem, can't create anything more vitalizing.

Here's the plan for the day. Lazy morning. Coffee. Some more lazy morning. Step out for a long brunch. A brunch so long and so beautifully inebriating that it practically beams you back to bed. Wake up only when it's time to drive Nat to the airport. This is what heaven wrapped up in an agenda looks like.

The plan got somewhat derailed at stage one. By the time I poured the coffee and carried it in, Natasha was already on a work call. Which turned into a two-hour video call. So we ate Chinese takeaway instead. Not the MSG-filled, cheap Chinese. But exquisite, tasteful, delicate Chinese from one of Natasha's favourite restaurants that does not offer takeaway, but does for us.

While Natasha worked, I stepped out for a run. While I ran I played back our dinner with her parents on Saturday night. Her mother wanted to know if we had a wedding date in mind. Her father thought there was no need to rush into things. Her mother felt long engagements were not the best idea. Her father felt that was old-fashioned thinking and there was no place for old-fashioned when we were talking about a young woman with a brilliant career and unlimited prospects in the twenty-first century.

We worked our way through the first course, listening to politely contrary views on the topic of our wedding plans. You have to hand it to her parents. They make everything so faultlessly civil, it's hard to figure they are in a constant state of disagreement on everything. But they were. I felt we were in two different rooms having two very different, but very sophisticated and flawlessly civilized, conversations.

By the time the second course arrived, Natasha laughed charmingly and dismissed their concerns and put a skilfully practiced end to their tennis rally backing and forthing with one simple comment, "Dad, Mom, we've got this."

For one brief moment I wondered if we did. It was just a fleeting, fast, faster than a sniper's bullet, thought. What if we don't have this? But of course we do. Nat's assignment will be over in seven months and we'll be perfectly on track to move on. Nat's got this. That's the thing about her. When she says she's got it, she's got it. She's the best living example of 'If the plan doesn't work, change the plan but never the goal'. The goal doesn't change. We're both goal-cracking Jedis. It's what we do best. We've got this.

I told her that. Seat 7B, that is. When she asked her twenty-fourth random question of the day. Or was it hundred-and-fourth?

"What are the three things that made you fall in love with your partner?"

I tell her there are way more than three. But she has these corny rules. "If you had to distil it down. Bare bones. Three. No more, no less."

"Well, one look at Nat and, you know, you can't ignore her looks. She's searingly hot. Two would be how she's hardwired for success. She doesn't play small. She sets a goal and kicks its ass."

"Okay, that sounds like six things but it's actually just two, so what's three?"

She's playing math teacher now? "Well, she's just great," I conclude.

"Kind of less generic, maybe?" And she's patronizing as fuck.

I mean there are a million things. Bazillion! Too many things to count that make Nat fantastic. She keeps on waiting for me to say something. I can not shake off the feeling that she is testing me. Or is she teasing me? She tilts her head in that annoying manner that seems to ask without asking, 'Are you travelling as an unaccompanied minor?' I am starting to hear stuff she doesn't even say. That's how loud her thoughts are. I love home court advantage. I detest being against the ropes.

"Great in bed. How's that for three?" Boom! Shake things up a little bit.

"Perfect." She doesn't bat an eyelid. If anything, she looks mildly underwhelmed. I feel like I've lost even before we are halfway through this ridiculous game of hers.

"So, hit me with yours," I say.

"It's his unshakeable belief that the world is a good place with mostly good people. He's so at ease with it. It percolates down to everything and everyone."

Of course it makes sense. Disney princess is married to Winnie the Pooh.

"Two. He's not into grand gestures—"

"How can that be a good thing?"

"He's into whatever the moment brings. Mad moments mostly. Every night when he takes the dog for his last walk of the day, he'll return with something. Something silly, something small, but something that has the power to transform into magic. It could be a twig that he claims looks like a constellation and is presented with a magician's extravagant flourish. Or it could be a tub of an oddly-flavoured ice cream. He'll walk in asking everyone to guess what's in the poo bag. Azaan, who's finished brushing his teeth and should be in bed, will scream, 'Doggie poo!' The little one babbles with the conviction that he's said exactly what his brother has. And the game goes on till the big reveal, after which it's pretty pointless protesting that nobody should be eating ice cream after brushing their teeth and certainly not little people who are going to be too sugar-rushed to sleep ever again."

That was only number two, that whole big story about nothing, that was only number two. She rambles off point to make a point. And what was the point here, anyway?

"Three. He's never in a hurry. To speak, to get ahead, to get it done, which can be an annoying thing, I admit, but it's such a good thing. When he's listening to you—he's really listening. And the thing is, he listens to a lot of people. He listens to everyone. The doorman, the babysitter, the kids. He's the guy, when you bump into at a coffee shop, will stop and give you all his attention if you tell him you're having a bad morning."

I shrug. She notices. "You don't get it, do you?" she asks.

"No, but knock yourself out. Clearly, these are things that do it for you."

"Think about it. Mostly when someone says I hear you, they're looking at a screen, or answering a call, or going over a mental job-list. I hear you has become code for let-this-conversation-be-over. Imagine what a gift it is to have someone give you their full attention because they really do want to hear you."

We're pulling up at JFK. Natasha, on the passenger seat, is engrossed in replying to an email. I ask her if she's still up for the long weekend trip to the Bermudas we talked about. She says, "Sure." But she hasn't looked up. I am wondering if she hears me.

Of course she does. She turns to give me a long kiss.

"Olive, Teal, Sky, Green, Fern, Star, Peony, Honey, Aspen, Willow. This year's most popular eco-friendly baby names!" Max reads them like they are devastatingly unmentionable words that will land us in a bottomless pit of despair if we repeat them more than once. "Seriously! We get that you want to give off a responsible green citizen vibe, but do we have to make it so damn faddy?"

"You forgot Goddess Beyoncé named her daughter Blue, and the famously uncoupled Gwyneth Paltrow has an Apple at home in the form of a daughter," José reminds her.

It may not sound like it, but we're actually in the thick of an official brainstorming session. We're talking about upping the ante with our blog. We aren't aiming to become the next Dot Earth, the *New York Times*' award-winning, serious, environmental issue-tackling, phenomenally hardworking blog, that set the bar just a notch higher than the sky. Our target audience is the average nature-loving seven-year-old who doesn't really need to read about the fact that Ikea is now selling home solar power systems or that a science curator sees hope in earth's Anthropocene Age. And even if the average kid's average mom and/or dad do happen to peer at the blog over their child's shoulder, all they want, really, is a bite-sized stockpile of facts to arm them to sound at least as smart as their kid at the dinner table. And while they are at it, they wouldn't mind seeing how the cool set do their bit of 'green living'. Think of it like the vicarious pleasure we get from flicking through a glossy magazine at the hair salon and spotting our favourite celebrity at airports, painstakingly put together to look almost ordinary.

We're researching the cool set right this minute. Instead of drowning us in a pool of idea-generating stimuli, the exercise is just making us laugh ourselves into a high level of inefficiency. Or, if you're Max, then it's just annoying the heck out of you with its obvious pretentiousness. "I hate that the hipster brigade is making environmental consciousness a gentrification thing for the haves."

I'm not sure I agree. I'm about to tell her that, but we have to keep in mind that a Max rant is the verbal equivalent of the 1883 eruption of Krakatoa. Only, Krakatoa had been dormant for two hundred years before initial rumblings began, followed by occasional venting and spewing that apparently lasted nearly three months before the catastrophic eruption. This would be factually and historically incorrect in the case of Max. She is never dormant or silent. Her eruptions and venting are anything but mild, but they are rarely prolonged and certainly never catastrophic.

Max isn't done—is she ever? "On one hand, they go waxing apocalyptic and then go off and create these silly hipster obsessions—avocado on toast—over which they go nuts until it becomes the new food emergency. Hey! Just pause for a moment before tapping your avocados for ripeness, and consider this—your avo fixation is causing illegal deforestation in Mexico." Small insight here might help: the present rant may have been exacerbated by the fact that Max happens to be currently seeing a (considerably younger) foodie who suffers from the fashionable avocado-at-least-once-a-day malaise. "Also, I feel like environmental awareness has been co-opted by the kale-chomping Bikram Yoga fanatics. Stop hijacking what's not yours to look new-effin-agey!"

José, self-appointed yuppie zeitgeist maestro, adds fuel to Max's fire. "Hipsters are now also suggesting one way of saving the planet is having fewer or no kids, each of whom creates fifty-eight tonnes of carbon dioxide a year." Before Max erupts once more, I manoeuvre the conversation to safer ground, or up in the air, actually. "Oh, really? My flying partner suggested that, although he's anything but a green hipster. It was more to annoy me, I suspect."

Max stops what she's doing. "You know this guy hasn't left you for a really long time . . ."

José joins her. "Yeah, I mean you dismissed him saying

he was a money-worshipping Wall Street type, and upon further drilling conceded he was chiselled-ish, but honestly, he's starting to sound way too cute."

I am completely glued to my laptop—cruising through competitive blogs, paying little attention to José and his inquisition. "Hardly cute. More like consistently exasperating. I had him pegged the minute he walked in with his Louis Vuitton suit bag."

"Confirmed!" José claps like thunder. "The ultimate romcom trope is loathe at first sight! And then we know how it pans out."

José, according to his résumé, is a thirty-three-year-old man, but his romantic inclinations have remained those of a thirteen-year-old girl's. Everyone, in his head, is living for one reason alone: that one crash-bang-cymbals-light bulb-aha!-romcom moment. It doesn't matter if you're a very married, hapless, juggling mother of two, or a wizened eighty-year-old war veteran. "Something happened there and he was definitely more than chiselled-ish." See. José isn't even pretending to work now.

"Okay. He wasn't exactly un-good-looking. More importantly, he was smug, contrarian, and flagrantly consumptive. His idea of beautiful rain is possibly sprinkling dollar bills like confetti from his penthouse balcony. I was trying to look after a baby while recovering from an evil tummy bug. That's what happened."

Both of them say nothing. Both of them have identical expressions of doubt. Both of them are waiting for coherent justification.

"Guys, there's me. And then there's this person whose idea of extreme austerity is giving up a Bentley for a Porsche. Maybe that's why he's still stuck in my head. Annoyed stuck."

The expressions of doubt persist, but we finally get back to the business of our blog. Only, in my head I don't. He would find our blog woefully inadequate and our present debate nothing short of vastly amusing. He would. Seat 7A. He just didn't get the point of what we do. The lack of scale! He's big on scale. He was swaggeringly condescending about all things that lacked scale. Anything!

"You have to know this one . . . How do Prius owners drive?" Does one even attempt to answer something so bafflingly stupid? He chuckles. Then gifts me the answer. "One hand on the wheel, the other patting themselves on the back!"

The look on his face, it's like he's hosting the Oscars and the entire room is giving him a standing ovation. I realize it's a harmless joke and I should smile. But what is it about him that makes me run into Clark Kent's booth and emerge as SuperKilljoy? "I can see why you'd find conservation funny. Wait, aren't you the guys who legitimized that whole subprime-mortgage crisis that brought the American middle class, actually the world, to its knees?"

He offers a kind smile, like I don't get it and never will, but his largesse will somehow get me through. "I'm just an oil trader. And that happened before I was anywhere close to Wall Street."

Nicely done. The foremost evangelist for the Wall Street

life absolves himself of the ways of his tribe. "Don't you all pride yourselves in the whole risk and reward thing?"

"Sure. Only those who have the brains and the balls to take the risks reap the life-changing rewards."

"Yeah, about that. I'm just going to go with Nicholas Taleb when he says we should ban banks from risk-taking because society is going to pay the price."

I know he wants to respond, but for some reason he chooses not to.

Just as well. This is not going anywhere. It never will. Azad is awake and wants to walk. When you're walking behind someone who's just learned how to walk, a short walk down an airplane aisle means only one thing: a reflex-sharpening marathon which ends with you looking like a spatially challenged primate. Oops, almost topples over, nearly there, no! no! no! That's a man's toe—not to be held for support. By the time we return, Seat 7A is thankfully immersed in his screen. Uh-oh. From the look on his face and the manner in which he's removing his headset, I can tell he has redeployed his mental resources during my short absence and is now all set to hit me with a suitable response.

"Tell me something, did you sell your kidneys for this seat?" In an act of incredible self-discipline, I stop myself from asking him a slew of terrible, terrible, non-politically correct questions about the state of his mental well-being. "Then you don't get to play the humble have-nots card. You're sitting in a very expensive seat."

Well. Should I tell him? The ticket was a gift from my mother's brother who insisted I be there for the wedding.

His son's wedding. No, that would be too much information. So all he gets is this. "Wait, I am not impervious to perks. I'm just not used to treating them like a ventilator that keeps me alive."

A Seven-Eleven Wednesday

I've never really figured out how someone with even a smidgen of mental acuity doesn't know better than to ask you for a favour after hoping to ruin your life for most of your life.

That would be my dad. His wife. And their son.

To be fair, the son, Sachin, can't be blamed. He was less of a co-conspirator, more of a wuss bystander. Stepmom, on the other hand, could make Poison Ivy look like a genial, hug-dispensing grandmother. Her route to world domination was to sweep the stepson out of the way and pave the path for the real son—like the frickin' Olympic motto 'Citius, Altius, Fortius', make him Faster, Higher, Stronger and glory will be theirs.

Now here we are. Me, well, I'm okay. They? Maybe not so much. They run a Seven-Eleven store and live in a forgettable neighbourhood in a forgotten part of Toronto. No skin off my nose until they get in touch after three lifetimes to hit me for what they call a 'loan' and I call short-term stiffing, long-term write off.

Sachin's in love with some rich Punjabi daddy's princess and to prove his mettle, Sachin would like to wear the crown of everyone's present-day favourite cliché: entrepreneur. The last time I met my dad and his cosy little family was at an uncle's funeral—the only adult who was kind enough to give me hope that I'd get out of the hell-hole that my stepmother called home. Mind you, that wasn't her worst violation. Acting like a high roller at a Vegas casino, she advised Dad to mortgage our humble but well-oiled dry-cleaning business against a loan. Clearly, she'd learned something they don't teach you at Harvard Business School, because she whipped out quite the strategy: managed to lose the store and the money, further downgrade my father's lifestyle, and saddle him with a lousy Seven-Eleven store instead.

In her latest charm offensive, she wants me to fund the real son's hare-brained scheme for the sole purpose of snagging a cute, rich wife.

After the morning trading session, I stepped out to grab a coffee and who do I see shuffling uncomfortably in the office lobby? My very own on-the-brink-of-entrepreneurship half-brother, Sachin.

I look at sweet-faced, fidgety, incapable-of-making-eye contact Sachin and the movie geek in me is already thinking *Rain Man*. Two (half) brothers, one of them an autistic savant. I'm not being rude here. Sachin has that whole vibe going on, sadly, without the brainpower. He keeps counting something invisible on his fingertips, looks everywhere except at the person he's talking to, and still manages to look like he might suddenly uncover a genius discovery. The only thing I'm about to uncover for him is the knowledge that he'll be on the next flight home minus any funding from me.

"Nice guys finish last is such a cliché." She, Seat 7B, has this unusual talent for meaningless statements by remembering something I said three hours ago in an entirely unrelated context. I'll admit I feel compelled to correct her naïve misgivings. "In case you hadn't noticed, the real world works like that."

"Maybe on Wall Street, where the phrase was, no doubt, coined, but I doubt if every single person is running your frantic race."

"No, the settlers aren't."

"Maybe they settle for something else, something much more important to them?" She's prompting me like a helpful teacher.

"Yeah, that's the kind of story people who don't make it tell themselves."

One thing, got to hand it to her, she doesn't give up. "Let's not go there. Everyone's idea of making it is always going to be dramatically, vastly, incomprehensibly different. What makes you is all that matters."

Here's my take. "For the A-Player, last year's world record is this year's starting point, so it is a race. Everything is."

"My problem with this race thing is we're all reduced to being rats—desperately scrambling and scurrying. As human beings, surely we can do better."

If that arbitrary statement isn't bad enough, I am then subjected to some New Age Buddha speak. "You know, all this talk about winning, racing, and chasing . . . I feel like people are just running . . . running away from something."

I've realized one thing, our conversations will never end. They can't. It's like we live in alien worlds, speaking unknown languages. "I'd like to believe I run towards something—it's called having a goal. Everything else becomes a cop-out," I say. She nods. Like she finally gets it. Whoa! This is a first.

Ten minutes later, she looks up from her sleeping son's face. "I think everyone's always running to forget, to cauterize pain, trying to cure ourselves of stuff as fast as we can—removing chunks of ourselves along the way. At some point, we all have to forgive someone or forgive ourselves. It helps us to stop running. You have to. It's just a matter of when. Not if."

This is nuts. What's to forgive? We're talking achievers and settlers.

I'm convinced she's addicted to some invisible pulpit where she stands and delivers meandering, meaningless sermons to anyone within earshot.

FYI, I did cut a cheque for Sachin. I mean it wasn't huge. Just a token. Okay, it was more than a token. The point is, it was done to keep him away. Them away. Sachin looked so damn dazed and confused. He also looked like he may cry. Anyway, done and dusted.

Just for the record, I don't forgive. Or forget. Never want to see them again. And damn right, I'll run as far as I have to—anything to get away from them.

The Kindness of Strangers Wednesday

It's the third day in a row that Riz and I have moved out of our bed, our bedroom, our safe space, to collapse—like our kneecaps have suddenly dropped out without warning—into Azaan's empty bed. Riz has a six am wake-up for a flight. I don't have that much: only the next four days without him, work, a tonne of writing deadlines, two boys, one dog, one consistently late nanny, two birthday parties, and appropriate gifts to be procured. The boys and the dog have ended up in our bed all week. It's mostly fun. Until you realize you're starting to feel like a ball of dough constantly being kneaded out of shape as various objects (limbs mostly) find a way to wedge themselves into you and startle you awake faster than a shrill alarm clock with no snooze button.

Doesn't help that Azaan has taken to asking probing—or are they philosophical?—

questions at a time when, according to sleep specialists, our bodies have turned into little factories for regenerating all good things. No problem for Riz. He sleeps like he's under general anaesthesia administered for a six-hour surgery. You could play the soundtrack of the most relentless war movie at Imax-theatre decibels and he wouldn't move or alter that annoyingly peaceful expression on his face. I wake up if a housefly rubs its forelegs together within a five-mile radius.

"When we re-pot a plant, does the roots get hurt?" Through my fugue state I catch myself wondering if I should play grammar Nazi (you mean, do the roots get hurt?) or just try to answer the question (they get a bit bruised, but if they are strong they grow out and don't feel anything) and hope it will put him and his questions to bed. While wondering the whole time if my son is way too sensitive if this is his only take-away from his first 'kinder gardening' class. I touch his little hand. I feel the thin, long scar running across his outer palm to the inside of his thumb. The subject of sleep deprivation slips into the backseat. The scar never fails to make me feel like my ribcage is contracting and disappearing. A jagged reminder of all the threads of frailty that are interwoven into our daily lives.

I remember feeling it on the plane. I remember asking him if he'd ever been touched by the kindness of strangers. I remember he looked at me with corrugated brows, like I'd tossed a Rubik's Cube at him, with a loud, ticking timer in my hands, and not a perfectly harmless question.

"I don't think I've depended on the kindness of friends or strangers or anyone, for that matter." Of course, he hasn't. A predictably swaggering Seat 7A response. "But clearly you have."

I tell him about this time Azaan, only two, had waddled into our bathroom and brought the glass shelf above the bathtub crashing down, and before I could pick him up, he picked up a tiny chard of glass that nearly sliced off his entire thumb.

Everything was a blur after that. The dangling thumb, the blood on the floor, on me, on Riz's white shirt, racing into the ER. I could only remember Azaan's beautiful little surprised face as the blood dripped all around. At first it was like he was taking it in, like it was happening to someone else, seemingly oblivious to what had to have been inconceivable pain. Uncanny silence. Then the unbearable explosion of gut-wrenching crying. The medics strapped him in a jacket to keep him from flailing; Riz carried him into the room where the surgeon had to stitch him up, insisting that I wait outside. It was summer. I was shaking like I was caught in a blizzard without clothes. "Without any warning, I was held in the arms of someone—the person gave me the longest, deepest hug I can ever remember receiving. I stopped trembling when I heard the words: 'He's going to be fine, absolutely fine. He'll brag about the scar.'"

"I know it was a woman. She had to have been a patient or someone she loved was. She was gone before I could see her face through the haze of misery and tears. Before I could ask her who she was. Before I could tell her how the hug saved me. Before I could forge a lifelong bond with her."

Seat 7A looked like he actually got what I had felt. Still felt. To his credit, he didn't say anything. Ask anything. Offer a sarcastic comment. Only this: "Did he start bragging about the scar?"

"He did. But before that, he did something else. Up until then he used to suck his right thumb, but when this happened he was thoroughly confused because he'd forget and take his bandaged thumb to his mouth. It made him stop sucking his thumb. Which is a good thing. But I have no idea why I felt more sad than relieved, like he'd been prematurely robbed of his favourite comfort. A forced growing up."

"See, I don't ever want to be hugged by a stranger—nah, not my thing—that's just violating my space." And he was back.

"I am not one to quote studies, but it's right there and it has to be said: we're suffering from a loneliness epidemic—men, even more than women. You just perpetuated that idea with this . . . this macho denial for comfort."

He shakes his head, smiles, stands up, bends over, displaying yet again an impossible degree of suppleness as he places his palms on the floor, then goes a step further and stretches both legs into an almost perfect split. I feel like it's the physical equivalent of the words 'Just shut up already'.

He settles back into his seat, looks at me with the gleeful expression of a kid looping through monkey bars. "So hugs are the way to reform despots and terrorists . . . Let's save the world one hug at a time and make Winnie the Pooh president."

Below Freezing Wednesday

I left the Cryo Zone Spa with my body feeling ten years younger and my mind swept clean of the morning's market volatility chaos.

Not one of my best trading days. Probably one of my worst. Then there was Larry, being Larry. Neurotic as fuck. Pathologically neurotic. Golf club-wielding neurotic. At least he didn't slam me against his office door, pressing his 9 iron to my throat. No, really, he does that. To use the perfect analogy, it's par for the course. I've had too many winning days, months actually, for him to pull his favourite nut job stunt on me. But Jason and Vikram got the five-star I-am-closing-your-books-and-bashing-your-balls treatment.

Larry can be your best cheerleader (when you close a million dollar trade) and the worst bully (when you drop the ball). He's fast. Takes him a split second to go from psychotic, genocidal maniac to suave big-bonus-signing mentor. The deal is to keep your cool. Keep your head. Know your shit. Learn to win big after you lose small. Jason's been losing big and winning very little. After the day's trade, Larry nearly gave him a colonoscopy with his golf club. I swear I thought Jay was going to bleed from his clenched fists.

The stress from a bad morning of quick typing, wrong calls, phone calls, screen sharing, and such seemingly sedentary shit can turn the body into something that's been pummelled by brass knuckledusters. A five-setter against Nadal at his peak. Chasing after LeBron James on the court for three days. Jogging barefoot through the Sahara.

One session of cryotherapy fixes everything in under five minutes. Un-ages you. Un-hackles you. Relaxes every bone in your body. "And this is your let-them-eat-cake moment?" No prizes for guessing. That was the voice of my closet socialist flying partner, Seat 7B, when I told her about the unending benefits of my recovery ritual.

"Isn't that what body and muscle battered athletes need?" She wants to confirm.

"Sure, I hear LeBron frequents the same spa. And I'm sure somewhere on the other side of the world, MS Dhoni has found a similar one. Look, it's just the twenty-first century version of the ice bath. A cryogenic chamber powered by air-cooled liquid nitrogen that envelopes your body and heals it in under four minutes. Just enough time to listen to your favourite EDM track. Or in your case, rain sounds or forest sounds."

My subtle sarcasm and the details of this awesome system of healing are tragically lost on her.

"I love how your tribe screw everyone over and then lean on prohibitively expensive pastimes to survive the trauma of being unfairly rich."

This beats hand-to-hand combat. But I've decided these bouts of mutually assured destruction have to be spaced out. I set a limit: no new attacks under twenty minutes. But then here I am, rearing to get back into the arena in less than ten. Dive into the next disagreement; all self-discipline, self-allocated time statutes abandoned. It's her fault! She's so effing Dame Judi Dench high and mighty about all things that don't involve rebuilding hurricane-hit towns. I ask, "You sound jealous, or is it bitter?"

She laughs. Okay, wasn't expecting that. "Actually, I'm neither. I love my life. Cherish my comforts. Clearly nothing like yours, but good enough for me. Not to say I don't have my own set of escape fantasies."

See, this is what she does. This ordinary, domesticated mother of two, save-the-world-preachy, completely impractical woman. She says things you don't expect her to. Things people rarely say out loud outside of an intimate friend circle. But her thoughts turn into specific words and slip through the barrier of polite formality without any warning. Her observations need the security of a firewall. It's the only way to protect perfect strangers from the risk of getting infected by her misplaced enthusiasm for all things stunningly unimportant. You get sucked into her crazy head. You want to see it through. Need to know how this is going to go down! Why did she say what she said?

"Escape fantasies?" I have to ask.

"Like when Starbucks puts the wrong name on your drink order. I always imagine it to be a portal to a new identity . . . it could take you anywhere—a career in organized crime, a covert operation, an artist's loft . . . Oh, the possibilities."

She shuts her eyes for just a moment longer than a blink. Giving the impression she may have gone down one of the above-mentioned rabbit holes.

"You must have them? Flights of fantasy?" She opens her eyes to ask.

I remember the untended patch of pathetic green we called a backyard when I was a kid. It was good for only one thing: to get lost in. Nobody bothered to come outside. Most months it was too cold. And when it wasn't covered in ice and snow, it was overrun with weeds. For some reason, no one ever thought of removing the enormous top-loading, non-functioning, discarded washing machine that just sat there for years. Perfect place to climb into and get lost. It was my anti-gravity chamber. My ride to the moon. My safe space.

"No. Don't have them. Never have. Only people who can't afford to live their dreams need fantasies. It's really that simple."

The way she's looking at me I feel like I've told an addict her dealer just died.

"How can you compare expensive spa treatments and

Bentleys with the power of imagination? Visiting places on old maps . . . discovering new worlds . . . stepping into unchartered territory . . . meeting bareback horse riders, and slaying dragons along the way?"

This is hilarious. "What are you? Six? Every adult knows that stuff only looks good on a high-definition television screen and a Bentley in real life beats all the magic in the combined franchise of all the Harry Potter books and movies put together."

This is it. It all boils down to perspective. And compromises. For most people, having fantasies is their escape from an unsuccessful reality. Work harder, already! That's all there is to it.

"Of course, go on, judge the entire world through your one per cent perspective." She thinks she has the last word. Not. On. This. This is what I do. This is my religion.

"Like Bobby Axelrod says, the moral of the story is you get one fucking life—do it all."

She shakes her head slowly, uncomprehendingly. "I'm afraid I don't know this New Age guru who sounds aggressively un-fun."

"Come on! Axelrod, from *Billions*!"

She smiles a victory smile. "Oh okay, and I thought *I* needed to get out of my make-believe world and get real."

Left Leaning Wednesday

What do Barack Obama, Fred Astaire, Leonardo Da Vinci, and a small sliver of the world have in common? They are lefties. Southpaws. Against-the-tide warriors. Since the beginning of time, right is, well, right. And left is ambiguous and, all too often, un-right. If that isn't bad enough, through the ages, being left-handed has worn the mantle of such flattering traits as sinister, clumsy, unlucky, evil, uncoordinated. Think of the unfairness of the simple phrase: Right is right. Read the subtext. It's saying lefties are wrong. The same guys who always have to try harder to fit in. Fit into a flipped opposite world. Maybe, that's why I lean towards them—an inbuilt de facto affinity for the underdog. Or the *left* out—happy to stoop to abysmal wordplay to make my point.

This afternoon's musing, or quasi-rant if you prefer, is brought on by the fact that I was the parent volunteer in Azaan's class today and I couldn't help but notice the invisible but subtle pressure on him, a natural lefty, to realign his body, his paper, his arm, to somehow fix the asymmetry of his left-handedness. The well-intentioned teacher kept helping the lefty kid to look more comfortable. Yes, when lefties write they can look awkward. Their left arm practically snakes right around the paper and the paper rarely sits straight. It's always skewed, sometimes three-sixty degrees, to facilitate whatever their idea of alignment might be.

It's not about Azaan. Okay, maybe just a little bit. Mostly it's how everything in the world, from door handles to tools, even the humble scissor, is placed to our right-handed advantage.

"Be ambidextrous—double your advantage." That piece of unquenchable optimism mingled with subtle mansplaining was from Seat 7A.

Be ambidextrous. Be infallible. Be titanium. Be a warrior. How about we give up posturing for maybe fifteen seconds and just exhale?

Let's just hold our little boys close and tell them it's okay to be themselves. And do it before the world gets to them and makes them believe they have an obligation to ceaselessly power through life like Olympic athletes. Anything less will toss them, unceremoniously, into this dreaded worse-than-hell category: sissy.

Obviously, Seat 7A did not get the memo on don't-be-that-guy. He explains, "Pro-tip. Resilience makes winners. Got a weakness? Work through it and make sure it never comes in the way of what you want."

See, we really do have to get to boys before they feel no qualms about spouting such alarmingly bad testosterone-injected clichés. Before they transform into perfectly engineered cyborgs with zero chinks in their titanium bodies and drained-of-humanity minds. Not to mention surgically-removed tear ducts—to avoid any instances of this unmanly thing called crying.

"Wait, I get it, any sort of vulnerability, and being a leftie therefore, nullifies the man card. So let's macho through!" I say.

"What does it take to get a job like mine? Analytical skills? Data crunching? Appetite for risk? That's just basic boring résumé stuff. Really, they only want just one thing: killer competitiveness. No room for weakness. You wipe out chinks. Like you wipe out anything and anyone that slows you down. So, to your point, if being a left-handed person gives you doubts—teach yourself to be right-handed. Don't expect the world to flip horizontally. Don't pander. Don't moan. Fix it. And win."

Seat 7A folds his arms across his chest, accentuating his perfectly sculpted upper body that looks buff with smugness under his still pristine white tee. To my credit, I am not laughing out loud, I am going through possible scenarios that could have brought on the enthusiastically delivered dribble disguised as a Nazi motivational speech: a) he's playing back a commencement speech made at a gladiator-training academy, b) this is actually sensational, self-deprecating humour and the punch line is on its way.

I find option two extremely appealing. I wait for my faith and humour to be restored.

"You know, I've actually chosen to go swim with sharks."

No, that punch line is not coming. Instead, I'm going to be treated to more ridiculously infantile stories of masculinity.

I shrug. "I imagine you do that for a living."

He grins. "Funny. But I meant real sharks."

Everything they say is true then. Men trying too hard to be men can be a ruinous pastime.

"It's not for everyone. But nothing makes you more resilient. When you start the swim, they let you know that the sharks haven't eaten anyone. But they can. Of course, they can. So if a shark starts circling around you, two things: don't emit fear, don't swim away—they'll come after you, rip you apart. If you think the shark looks hungry, there's only one thing to do, gather all the strength in your body, resolve in your mind, and punch it in the face. Surprisingly, it scares the shit out of them. They just swim away."

And we are back. Hovering somewhere between Darwin's Homo erectus and Homo neanderthalensis creatures of evolution.

"Kicking the crap out of anything that can undermine you is the only fuel you need to go places."

This brand of schoolyard bully conviction makes any argument moot. Is there even any point in trying to tell

Seat 7A that the world is not a balance sheet for measuring strengths and weaknesses? Nope. But I do want to ask him something.

"Tell me something, you kick the crap out of all weaknesses, but what about love, relationships, caring, family, friends . . . Some might argue they are weaknesses too?"

He shrugs. He's got this. Like he's got everything else.

"I look at it like I look at my trades. There are upsides. And downsides. If the downsides start exceeding the upsides, just walk away."

I am certain I can hear dead gladiators applauding in their graves.

"By the way, did you know that Michelangelo created the Sistine Chapel ceiling despite being left-handed? Silly man, never thought to demolish his weakness and double his advantage."

This hangs in the air. Then looking like a patchwork of pride, bravado, and faint embarrassment, he lets me know, "Well, I guess that's exactly what I did—went from left-handed to ambidextrous."

Duct Tape Wednesday

Hate him. Love him. Or laugh your guts out at his audacity to declare he wants to run for the most powerful office in the world. But you can't ignore the fact that Kanye West knows what he's talking about when he raps, 'This the life that everybody ask for.' Feign satisfaction all you want with your Buddha quotes—'If you love the life you have, you have everything you need.' Wait. Hell, no! Admit it. You want the good life. Own the finest, be the coolest, live in a world where access to everything is a given—the uncomplicated rewards of no-worry money.

So here's the thing. I am never going to be pissed that Natasha and I are missing our calendar invites to meet in New York and/or Paris. We are doing the jobs that give us what we love and if you have to postpone a few life things along the way, well then, so fucking what?

See, that's why I love *Entourage* so much. It's a show that hits home with every geek, jock, banker, trader, and basically anyone with a Y chromosome who knows what every bro knows: you can't have enough of the good life! Now, if you haven't worked hard enough to get yourself that life, then there's eight seasons of wish-fulfilment to pretend you have. But if, like some of us, you have the smarts and the balls to get that life, then damn, you don't let it go. Even if the market and all its forces are playing tug of war with your trades. Today, it's tug of war with a spike-encrusted rope. Everyone's bleeding. Didn't help that OPEC pledged to cut supplies, causing an immediate spike in oil prices. Despite that, I've had an even sort of day. Which should be counted as a total win-win on a day like this. My book is looking as good as it did with the opening bell. Thanks to the intense discipline of my competitive-strategic-gambling brain and my trade-punching fingers being in disciplined sync.

Larry was like a walking compilation of Mike Tyson's angriest moments. He stopped next to Roger and I swear I could almost see the cortisol pumping through Roger's bloodstream—fight or flight, fight or flight, fight or flight was throbbing through the protruding vein on the side of his head. His numbers were slipping faster than a barefoot skier on a sharp slope. He was buying, selling, jabbing buttons, and absolutely nothing was working. He just kept losing but he didn't want to stop, the gambler's instinct had kicked in—I'll win it back on the next one. Larry brought out the duct tape and taped his right arm to his chair. That's what you get for being trigger-happy. Public humiliation and a practical lesson in holding your horses. Or as Larry said in a barely audible but distinctly ominous voice, "Calm the fuck down."

"Happens all the time. I had a boss who kept an electric roulette in the middle of the room. The type that has slots for five fingers. You place your finger in the wrong slot and a shock jangles through your body. It's a popular freshman drinking game—you get to pick from five slots and only one of them gives a shock, five to one odds. The shock is mild and the punishment involves knocking back a whiskey shot. Less trick more treat, really. On our trading floor, every slot was made to shock. Shocks of varying bludgeoning degrees. It was a Pavlovian lesson in learning to curb your trigger-happy fingers."

Seat 7B looked at me with a mix of sympathy and horror that I imagine a freshly-minted scientist has for a lab rat. "And this savage, psychotic treatment is all part of a day's work?"

I shrug. "Tough days. Happens to people around you. May or may not happen to you."

"And you're okay with this?"

I shrug. It's fun seeing her react.

"It's barbaric."

I shrug. This is really good fun.

"Debasing."

I shrug. This is even more fun than I imagined it would be.

"How can you condone something like this?"

My shrug feels like a well-targeted drone—landing a

fresh blow each time and rattling her Disney-mind out of shape.

"So I have an even better story. A female colleague had a breakdown after a lousy trading day and rushed into the conference room to gather herself. My boss kicked the door open and went, 'Just don't stain my carpet with those damn tears.'"

I feel like I've delivered the knockout punch. She is stunned. No more touchy-feely TED talking, hug-the-world better advice. She's done.

"This is like a horror anthology."

Apparently, she's not done. She's going to guilt me into giving up my million-dollar bonus?

"This flouts every rule of human decency and dignity. How do these people live with themselves?"

Hate to burst her bubble, but, "Quite luxuriously, actually. And with the help of some parasympathetic breathing. Calms the nervous system."

"It's like you're all stuck in reverse—an ode to caveman masculinity."

Of course she doesn't get it. She doesn't live in the real world. She doesn't breathe rare air. Now she's probably imagining we whip off our suits, replicate the sumo wrestler stance, slap our thighs, and charge at one another after each trade. Need to clarify.

"There's a cost to everything. As long as what you're getting in return is higher in value than what you're letting go, you're winning. And isn't that the point of life?"

She stares at me uncomprehendingly. You know, she

seems to do that a lot. Especially before she's about to deliver a cliché about being selfless and good.

"So this is your template for happiness."

Why is it important to me to win this? Maybe because winning is the point of life. Or maybe because I want her to know there's more to life than her doves of peace floating in the air while perfect children smell of baby powder. Life is ugly and hard. And only one thing buys you the freedom of choice: success.

Tossing fair play out of the window, I go for the jugular. "Do you have special shoes?"

She squints at me like she can't see who's talking in the dimly lit cabin.

"I mean you must. To navigate this tough terrain of moral high ground you spend your life on."

She smiles. She doesn't say it, but I think I hear the words 'Cheap shot'.

Jet Trail Wednesday

I'm all for laissez-faire. My nanny can be a cross-dressing communist, but just let her show up on time and leave her beliefs at home. On most days, she just about manages one of the two, with considerable difficulty, accompanied by loud Bollywood music streaming from her smartphone. Today she's late, on the phone, and gesturing she may need to leave in a few minutes. She got here twenty minutes ago and has been on the phone for fifteen of those minutes. I'm already mentally rearranging my workday while trying to get Azaan to *drink* his cereal and start tying his shoelaces when Nanny hangs up and tells me she's on Shaadi.com. If we linger, Azaan will be late for school. I nod enthusiastically at her as I herd my boy towards the door. Shaadi.com, Match.com, Tinder . . . go for it. Just let me know a day before you're taking the day off.

And then she tells me why she's taking the day off. A suitor from Amritsar, via Shaadi.com, is to be met this afternoon. I feign excitement with an enthusiastic but economical 'wow' while I slot my future employee worries in a to-do-later box and head for the door. Azaan stops halfway to stare out of the window. He refuses to move. Really? Now?

He points at something and then I see it. A perfect jet trail in a perfect cerulean sky. He looks back at me to confirm, "Nanu?" I nod. Now we both stare out of the window.

Grief invokes the strangest coping mechanisms. Most of all, the unconscious but constant searching for signs from the one gone missing. Anything to make us believe our grief isn't unrequited.

Baba was never meant to go so fast. But he did. No fuss. No mess. He was the life of the party one minute, the light of my life every single day, and gone the next. Too young to go, they said. Too spectacular to go is what I say. The ordinary could never be ordinary in his presence. He gilded everything with grace. He was touched with something that glowed so bright it could light up the night of a lunar eclipse. Baba and I loved our self-curated game of Top Five. So, in the spirit of things, if I had to name five things about him off the top of my head: exuberant curiosity, wonder, laughter, never-ending hugs, and an inexplicable love for Carl Sagan. All his questions were about the endless beyond. His best answers came from looking up at the sky. 'Never waste a minute being sad when you have all this beauty to look up to,' he would say while pointing at a full moon or a star-studded black sky, a forest of clouds, or what he called a pink gin sunset.

Ma was (is) a superwoman, superwife, and supermom, well before the term became an aspirational job title. She ran one of the largest non-profits in the country, which had to have been a cakewalk compared to keeping track of dreamers like Baba and me. She did it effortlessly and with just the perfect dose of humour and feigned frustration. Ma was a pro. Nothing could put a crease on her brow or on her ineffably cool starched cotton sarees. Still can't. Even a day after we had the prayer service for Baba and the house was swarming with well-meaning family and friends, Ma was the picture of serenity and dignified control.

"I discovered a birthday card in the form of a letter which my father had written to give me five days later on my sixteenth birthday. I was gutted before I found it. But once I read Baba's words in his exquisite handwriting, I was completely obliterated."

Seat 7A sits very still. Like he hasn't heard me. I know he has. The cabin lights are dimmed, window shades are down, and there is just the slightest hum of the engine. We are moving at the speed of sound. A few minutes earlier, I stood up to relieve a cramp in my foot and pushed up the window shade on my side. It turned out to be a secret portal into a seraphic universe. We were suspended between a flawlessly symmetrical sheet of white clouds below and dark skies above. A picture book half-moon looked spellbound, watching over a million stars, sparkling and resplendent, against what had to have been a jeweller's black velvet case.

I felt my heart expand with untold joy and intolerable sadness. The beauty of what I had just seen, and the nearness to Baba. I felt it all in that one moment.

I turn back and realize Seat 7A has also been looking outside and now he is looking at me. He has seen exactly what I saw at the exact same time. He witnessed the moment I felt intensely close to Baba. He obviously doesn't know it but I do, and maybe that's why it becomes as natural as breathing to talk about it. "My dad, he had a thing for the skies and all that lay beyond."

He says nothing.

That's when I tell him about the card.

He says nothing.

"When I found the card I left the room, the well-meaning friends and family, even Ma, and stood outside our house, crushed with sadness, unable to breathe. When I looked up at the sky, his sky, I saw this endless, long white jet trail streaked across a bright blue sky."

He says nothing.

"I knew it was Baba. I knew I was going to be okay."

Nothing. He is never going to say anything again. Fifteen minutes, and what feels like fifteen years later, he turns to me with a frown of confusion.

"I can't decide if it's worse to carry the load of crazy sadness from losing a parent or the one that comes from knowing you'll never miss a parent you'll lose."

It is a question for the books. But I already know the answer with every fibre of my being. "It has to be the latter."

Grand Slam
Wednesday

I t's my birthday today. Leo the lion, ruled
by the sun. Born to rule the world.

It's as if the trading Gods knew. I made
a killing. Obscene killing. Larry was practically
genuflecting when he came to wish me. It
looked like he was about to go all movie
moment on me: *Everything the light touches shall
be yours, my son.* The guys insisted we head to
the Knickerbocker Hotel for cocktails and
cigars. When we enter, we run into a rash of
tennis pros in for a promotional event for next
week's US Open. Jay looks so lit (first time in
weeks) he isn't going to need the tequila shots
that the others are already ordering in double
digits. Jay's a crazy-ass tennis fan. He prays at
the altar of Spain's Raging Bull, Rafael Nadal.
And his little guy, Joshua, despite his autism,
is like a million light bulbs when he watches
the game. So a few weeks ago I bought Jay and

Josh tickets for the finals. Tickets for the finals of the final grand slam of the year. My birthday give-back to him. And no, I didn't do it because of what she said.

"What do you like most about birthdays?" Seat 7B asks in her never-ending quest to run the world dry of questions before the end of our flight.

I tell her I don't care. Birthdays don't matter one way or another. Never have. Don't get what all the fuss is about. Besides, my life is already an all-you-can-eat buffet.

"I like the part about gifting back."

This has to be another shot at sainthood or guilt, yeah, guilt for getting gifts and too much attention on any one day. "I get it, you need to even it out because you feel guilty about getting stuff?"

"Haven't you been to a birthday party as a kid? The best part of it all is the return gift! Why do we stop doing that when we grow up?"

And then she embarks on yet another verbal detour because how can she possibly make a point without making twenty-two unscheduled stopovers?

"Everything gets drabber and unfunner if you only always follow protocol. Do you really have to go to the temple to pray or a club to dance? I read something wonderful that sums it up for me . . ." Pregnant pause till I've aged to my ninetieth birthday.

Then she remembers she was making a point. "Airports see more sincere kisses than wedding halls, the walls of hospitals have heard more prayers than the walls of churches and temples."

She looks at me like I should be applauding her for her latest non-epiphany. Frankly, I don't even get it. "And what's that got to do with birthdays?"

"Can anything be more fun than surprising the people you love with gifts on your own birthday?" She smiles as she remembers something. "I'll admit it turns into a bit of a problem when my older boy takes it literally and wants to gift half his school elaborate gifts on his birthday . . . but you get the idea . . . it's simply about saying this day would be nothing without you."

For what it's worth, I'm gifting myself to Natasha this weekend in Paris. But for now, I have just stopped by at Atillio's. He gives me a slice of his ragingly cool tiramisu with an espresso. I give him a box of Bolivar cigars.

Happy Birthday to me.

Eid Mubarak Wednesday

Riz has so much extended family between New York and Boston, I feel like if they stood shoulder to shoulder, they could cover the length and breadth of the Interstate-95. Fortunately for all concerned, they only emerge once a year to congregate as a unified whole. Don't get me wrong, I do like them and even love some of them. Justifiably more than Riz himself does. I'm almost certain he doesn't know the names of any of the newly added spouses and most of the kids. That's what comes from slyly dropping out of the family WhatsApp group, populated by thirty-five members of your perpetually burgeoning family. Needless to say, I'm still in the group. Admittedly, only politely active, but always on high alert for the butterfly effect. Someone sneezes in Arizona and I have to be aware it might, somehow, end with check-ups in

New York a month later, resulting in a sudden influx of unscheduled house guests.

The big question, asked in genuine bewilderment by Riz himself (who, like breathing, welcomes the world with open arms) is why I never opt out of the *atithi devo bhava* mode. His knowledge of Sanskrit is limited to tossing this phrase, or his self-coined handy acronym ADB, as a satirical poke at me. Implying I adhere to the ancient code from the Hindu scripture to treat all guests as God. My response to that is usually the non-verbal equivalent of: hold that thought, I haven't as yet formulated a presentation-worthy argument. But the doodle version of it is: I am a sucker for connection. In some convoluted arm-winding-from-the-back-of-the-neck-to-hold-the-ear way, I feel like my children need to know that we are connected to people who come in odd sizes and shapes. And when they learn to embrace them, it will somehow give them a sense of history, while it has to expand their hearts. Tall order for a toddler and six-year-old? But didn't someone say our children are the perfect thumbprints of our thoughts and actions? I could have just made that up. It sounds like me. It sounds like me trying to add heft to a losing argument. Most of my arguments, as you might have guessed, are with Seat 7A.

"So you don't have family in America but your husband does?"

I simply say, "Technically. But I think that just means we have family in America."

He shakes his head. "You're actually opting for something that most people want to shake off?"

There's this notion that the universe brings people into our lives for a reason. The notion is now cemented with brick and mortar into my brain, all thanks to this man. I know I'm spending these fifteen hours with him for several reasons: a) to stockpile my reserves of patience, b) to throw sleep and self-preservation to the winds and use all my energy and brainpower to convert him from being a strutting pre-schooler to some version of a thinking-feeling adult, and c) to earn industrial-strength willpower by resisting the temptation to resort to opiates within two minutes of starting a conversation with him. Any conversation about anything.

"When my kids see thirty-five people, often with mixed-race partners and children, celebrating Eid, it sets an example of how being Muslim is as myriad and varied as it is to be human."

He looks at me. "Didn't realize you were—"

"Muslim? Am not. My husband is. Although sometimes I'm not sure he is either."

"So why do you feel compelled to make your children see the light?"

I feel like there's a huge dollop of cavalier sarcasm there, but mostly it's the sum total of complete lack of understanding. So I try again. "Because when we are genuinely connected to other people, we become better people?"

"Oh wait, so practicing a religion, which is not your religion, is the way you teach this to your children?" Sometimes it's really impossible to tell if a person is being deliberately obtuse or has had entire hemispheres of their brain shut down from the pursuit of wealth and position. My problem is I respond to such people in entirely the wrong way: by over explaining what should never have to be explained in the first place.

"I don't care about religion. Heck, am not even sure if I believe in God. But I love to be part of anything that brings people, happiness, food, and generosity together. Be it Christmas, Diwali or Eid. I don't think it's my place to drill into my kids what religion, if any, to follow. I think it's my place to show them that the only way to live in this world is by not being suspicious of other peoples' choices."

He smiles at me like my entire existence till this point has been spent in a catatonic mist. "You know I love movies. Those lines you just said? Perfect for Tom Hanks or Denzel Washington. But in the real world . . . you do realize there's a logic flaw in that plan?"

I scarcely have the time to blink in incomprehension when he tosses this rare insight at me. "Have you not been living in this world? Suspicion is the new currency. Especially being suspicious of people like your children."

There is a wondrous array of wrongs in this sentence. Despite that, or perhaps because of that, I don't feel offended. It makes me realize this person, who is only cleverly disguised as an adult, requires the untiring persistence of a good grade school teacher. "See, you get it," I say. "That's why the only defence we have against such a world is to nurture children who can learn and teach kindness."

He wants to say something. Continue to throw guard-yourself truisms combined with practical survival techniques at me. Teach me a thing or two about the real world. Laugh in my face. Ridicule my naïveté. Instead, he just looks at me and smiles—saying without saying that I'm going to have to live and learn.

It makes me wonder what he might say if he saw the scene in our home right this minute. It is a potluck and food is the least of what makes it that. Vegans, vegetarians, the gluten-liberated, the dairy-intolerant, serious meat lovers, Indian Americans, Pakistanis, one Japanese, half a Mexican, a sprinkling of very white Americans, grumblers, greeters, huggers—celebrators ranging from age two to age eighty-one—are feasting together. We are all related. Although, a lot of us would likely fail the test if we were asked to explain exactly how. We might even kill each other if we had to do this more than once a year. But for now, everyone hugs, eats, and says Eid Mubarak (even if that's the only Urdu they speak), and means it.

I'm ready to sleep standing up at the door by the time the last of them leave. Riz is walking Azad back to sleep, I go to check on Azaan.

He's not ready to turn in just yet. He's converted my mother-in-law's prayer rug into a magic carpet. She sits on the floor with him, discussing possible destinations. He's talking intergalactic flight path. My father would give his resounding approval to that.

It works for me, Seat 7A. It's exhausting, it's mad, and it spreads me paper thin. But it works.

No Jargon
Wednesday

Time Value - check
Contango - check
Backwardation - check
Refinery Activity - check
Credit - check
Logistics - check
HSE - check
Equity - check
Spot Price - check
Brent - check
Arbitrage - check
Ad Valorem - check
ANOA - check
Absolute Bottom Sample - check
ACAOP - check
Accelerated Payment - check

All of the above, plus a book full of others, is the language I excel in. I speak it with proficiency. With conviction. I use it to my advantage. If this were a branch of linguistics, I'd be its aficionado. Its walking, talking, breathing mnemonic. Spanish, Portuguese, French, Italian, Romanian, and Catalan can go ahead and be self-congratulatory for their stature of Romance languages. This, right here, is the language of battle. Every oil trader speaks it. I've imbibed its subtle nuances; I know exactly how to harness its titanic power.

Other traders who work with shares or currencies depend on analysts and computerized trading systems. An oil trader needs to get into the trenches and speak the vernacular—speak to everyone, from journalists to people on the ground all around the world—get a fix on what's going down. Wars, global warming, too much rain, too little rain, typhoons, elections, and despots who don't want elections—everything impacts the price of oil. Everything impacts the oil trader. Comprehending the constant babble puts you in a position to call the shots.

So on a day when market volatility makes prices rise and fall by unnecessary dollars per barrel, you've got to hear what's being said. You translate it: buy aggressively or sell cleverly, the real skill lies in not getting lost in translation.

And when I close my book, up by half a million, on a volatile day, I know one thing for sure: this is my language of love.

"So what's your favourite number?" When Seat 7B asks a question like that, you have to know what an exercise in futility it is to explain to her that numbers are irrelevant when you have the power to make the most of whatever number you're given.

"Seen a movie called *21*?

She hasn't. Once more it's my job to enlighten her.

"It's about these six MIT students trained to become experts in card counting and then they rip millions off Vegas casinos."

Looking at me like cabin pressure has robbed me of all my mental faculties, she picks up the diaper bag and her son and heads for the toilet. This time, without the need for assistance. Thank God.

When she returns, she gets busy setting out some sort of baby food banquet—made up of an assortment of miniature bottles with miniature spoons to match. The toddler downs what looks like peach preserve and then gets going on something that looks like a bright green crayon mashed to pulp.

"Peas and spinach," she lets me know.

He doesn't like it so much and decides to spit it out. She uses a wet wipe to grab the slithery globule before it slides down his bib and spreads like an evil amoeba. At this moment, if Kahlil Gibran himself descended into the cabin to explain the poetic beauty of children, I'd laugh myself hoarse. And to prove me right, out pops another green globule from the toddler's mouth. She cuts the operation short. Disposes off the bottles, spoons, bib, used wipes et al. into a garbage bag, props the green globule-spewing monster on her seat, places a rubber picture book contraption in his hands, and rings for assistance. Once the garbage bag is cleared and the toddler is cooing at the toy in his hand, she turns to me. "Why would you start giving me the synopsis of an obscure movie when you could have just picked a random number?"

"Because it's never about a random number. So this guy, Ben, in the movie says: 'I had a 1590 on my SAT. I got a 44 on my MCATs. And I have a 4.0 GPA from MIT. I thought I had my life mapped out. But then I remembered what my Nonlinear Equations professor once told me, always account for variable change.'"

She looks baffled. "You memorized this whole dialogue verbatim? Really? It matters that much?"

"First, photographic memory—so it's not a big deal. What is a big deal is the idea of understanding what makes numbers click and using that to your advantage. In this case, variable change. The guy demonstrates how he can take a thirty-three point three per cent chance of winning and turn it into a sixty-six point six per cent chance by using the theory of variable change—it's potent stuff!"

She shakes her head and shrugs. Looks like I lost her about fifteen minutes ago.

"Seriously? You have to theorize and jargonize even the simplest questions until you strip them off all semblance of romance?"

"Romance? How does that even enter the picture, you're talking favourite numbers?"

"Romance, whimsy, small joys . . . I mean call it anything you want. Just don't science the shit out of it."

I have absolutely no idea what she's going on about. But then a quote I saw etched on the mirror in the toilet of a cool bar, jumps to mind: An intelligent man is sometimes forced to be drunk to spend time with his fools. If Hemingway can do it, let me give it a shot.

"So what's your favourite number and why?"

Thought you'd never ask is the only way to describe the look on her face.

"Three."

"Why? Why three and not two? Or zero? Or twenty-five?"

"I've heard mathematicians say zero is an astounding discovery; it's loved and glorified, nothingness and the beginning of everything. Two is super useful—it brings order—it is supremely eloquent at division. And then there's three. Which they believe wasn't actually needed. Which makes it a whimsical outlier in my book. A creativity-inspiring underdog. I also have three boys in my life. Three. Everything about it . . . makes it feel like it's mine."

Hemingway was so right. I need to be drunk senseless to make sense of this completely random line of thinking.

"It's like having a favourite day. Or a favourite colour. It defies logic. But the lovely thing is, once it's yours, you keep adding reasons for why it's yours, and then it takes on this magical quality. You almost want to celebrate it."

No wait, I have to get this out of the way. "Celebrate a number?"

"Celebrate a day, a number, a street . . ."

A day. "Okay. I celebrate any day when the numbers on my trading book climb in the right direction."

She shakes her head like *she*'s five years old.

"No. You can't have caveats. It's got to be your

favourite day from the start. It's special already. My favourite day is Wednesday. It's not the start of the week. It's not a flamboyant Friday. It's not the revered weekend. And yet, this humble mid-week day has this halo around it. I feel like nothing bad can ever happen on a Wednesday."

Yeah, right. It's Wednesday today. And look what I have to sit through.

Thor Wednesday

The nanny declares there will be no follow-up meetings with the gentleman from Amritsar. I perform a series of ecstatic somersaults of relief in my head. Then chide myself for my acute selfishness and make a suitably appropriate commiserating face accompanied by the right level of interest in this matchmaking non-development. The Shaadi.com suitor has been swatted out of her life like a fruit fly; although, I am still not sure I've grasped the parameters of her unequivocal rejection. She simply declared he looked like a friendly ape with the voice of Sachin Tendulkar. This information was disseminated as she fed Azad his breakfast and tapped one foot to an oddly rude-sounding track streaming from her phone. Apparently, the track is performed by a gentleman who goes by the name of Yo Yo Honey Singh. She makes it a point to inform me that he, too, is a son of Punjab. Do I now get how cheated she feels on the suitor voice front? Despite my most empathetic intentions, I'm not sure I do. Do all suitors have to pass the Yo Yo bar of voice capabilities? Why? We are listening to a string of disjointed, unrelated words held together by an autotuned voice that could be a robot experiencing agonizing pain—if robots felt pain.

What I do feel though, is an abiding sense of gratitude towards the rejected suitor and autotuned Yo Yo. Thanks to these men of Punjab, I can now get on with my workday and rush for my meeting to the Whaling Museum in Long Island—dive into this full day event organized by us, titled, not surprisingly, Whale You Save Me. I kiss Azad's head and try to wrap him in a cuddle before I leave, but I can tell he wants me to be done with it. Of course, I'm thrilled there isn't any evidence of separation anxiety, not even a pinhead. He hasn't stopped moving his head and smiling at the nanny, totally in the groove with her Yo Yo streaming. I'm thrilled. But I feel just the tiniest stab of infidelity. Note to self: must get the nanny to play more age-appropriate music.

Riz and I have mixed and matched our work schedules to ensure he's the one to take over from the nanny in the evening as I am likely to be immersed in telling our young participants why the endearing humpbacks need more warriors to save them. I am not a fan of the commute from Long Island at rush hour. A few days ago, I had bookmarked a talk on the possibility of teleporting. I wish I had watched it. I must watch it. And the other eleven hundred diligently bookmarked things for later reading and watching. Someday. Someday. Someday!

Going through mental lists can be empowering (evidence of a plan) and deeply demotivating (one step forward, hundred steps not taken!).

Watch the talk.

Mani-pedi - soonest.

Coffee morning with Azaan's grade moms - hmmm . . . hmmm . . .

Azaan's haircut - yesterday!

Azad's future playschool tour - *groans*

Learn to teleport - someday.

Find a less erratic-dramatic-matter-of-fact-foot-tapping nanny - yeah, right. Sissy.

My tomorrow's to-do is no competition for my someday (probably never) list. So here's the thing about someday that I can never decide. Is it a lie? Is it unfettered hope? Is it never? Is it postponed disappointment?

"It's nothing but procrastination." I can still hear Seat 7A's voice in my head. The high priest of crazed-with-ambition has spoken.

"I don't get postponing what you want. Create a tight bubble of complete focus and just nail it. What's stopping anyone?"

Nothing when someone only navigates the world from his carefully curated bubble.

"I'd like to start my day with a hundred *surya* namaskars

and go to bed at night with the knowledge that I have Ryan Gosling's immortal love, but real life does have a knack of getting in the way."

He's got the look. Like he's going to give me the codes to the nuclear warheads.

He sticks out a downward facing palm and says, "Life is this." Then raises the palm higher than his head. "I like this."

I can't put my finger on which movie, show, celebrity he's quoting, but it's got to be one of those fictional alpha men he talks about like they were his monozygotic twins.

"Those who really want it, like really want it, don't make lists. They make it happen."

Since we're in the vicinity of entertainment figures, I recall a character in *Wolf of Wall Street* who uses the power of literal chest-thumping and chanting—some sort of native war cry of greed. It wouldn't surprise me in the least if Seat 7A would be that person who wakes up and undertakes that peculiar ritual, sans irony, with unmatched religious fervour.

"Right, I'll just pencil that in and get to it later and fix my life."

He doesn't get it. This person whose body composition is fifty per cent muscle and fifty per cent arrogance, has no room for irony. "See, I have a zero tolerance policy for procrastination. I don't get people who postpone goals."

Don't succumb. Don't offer an authentic point of view. Repeat after me: don't succumb.

"Did it ever occur to you that some people love

something about where they are right now so much, they don't get caught up in the chase for future goals?"

"What's more important than getting where you want to be?"

I can think of a million things that are more fun and less tedious than running a never-ending race towards a perfectly chalked out life. "Like making a paper fortune teller."

He looks like he's been thwacked on the head. Twice. I ring for the flight attendant and request for a piece of paper.

He stares in fascinated confusion as I cut the A4 paper into a square and proceed to fold it—with my muscle memory, I could do this under heavy sedation—and within minutes, I'm using my index fingers and thumbs to open and close the rudimental origami-inspired fortune teller. The same one that makes every kid since the beginning of time a gleefully manipulative crystal ball reader. "So these four flaps have colours, you pick a colour, then move it around and stop at the numbers, you pick one, and then you get to look under the flap and it tells you something you may or may not want to know."

Clearly, Seat 7A, between three hundred push-ups and future wealth acquisition goals, has missed what I believed was a ubiquitous, no, *mandatory* childhood pastime. For now the argument fizzles out. He's just too confused by my reaction to react.

I reach after a twelve-hour absence to a frighteningly neat and spookily quiet home. I head instinctively towards the kids' rooms. Both are sound asleep. I bend over to kiss Azad, expecting pieces of caked baby food to accost my skin along the way. He smells deliciously clean and baby shampoo-edible. Azaan, wound into a perfect ball, has his head tucked impossibly close to his chest. He's a light sleeper. I can never risk kissing his head or tucking the blanket around him—his eyes are known to fly open and not shut till a few hours later. I kiss him within a hair's breadth, literally. His hair smells of grape shampoo, a new favourite of his.

As I tiptoe out of his room, I hear hacking that can only be someone smashing their way through the front door or maybe an entire kitchen counter. The latter is a more accurate guess. Riz, armed with a hammer (a tenderizer, technically), is smashing through a large brick of frozen biryani. The kitchen is a picture of post-apocalyptic debris and shrapnel wasteland. He turns around and smiles like he's just found me after a long search. "Honey, you're home!" He never tires of this tired joke. He delights in it so much it never seems to get old.

"We were supposed to continue our meeting into dinner, but I told Roberto and Varun here that we make the best biryani in North America. Plus there's always chilled beer in the fridge." I turn to my left and see his colleague-friends seated at the small kitchen table, armed with a Corona each, which they raise in greeting as they walk towards me.

Technically, we don't make the biryani. Riz's mom does, in vast quantities. We're really proficient at freezing it and, some of us, at defrosting it. Riz brings down the hammer again and this time the biryani brick splits in half, sending one portion flying from the counter straight into the kitchen sink where bits of it begin to disintegrate over unwashed dishes.

Riz turns to me, hammer in hand, funny smile on his face. No, he's nothing like Thor. Not a trace of Chris Hemsworth's deliciousness wrapped in Norse mythology. He's just Riz, childlike elation and a joy-now junkie. "*Ande ki bhurji* and hot buttered toast is almost as good as my mother's biryani, right?"

Muay Thai
Wednesday

According to the Pareto principle, eighty per cent of the results come from twenty per cent effort. In Muay Thai—kickboxing—this is just as true, but nothing's tougher than getting to the twenty per cent that works for you. I sweat bullets over technique, timing, and focus, which basically means I am nowhere close to reaping the end benefits of functional fitness and muscular endurance. Not fair? I love that life is unfair! It's a straight up advantage that I was born to milk. Look, a small percentage of us at the firm account for the largest chunk of the profits. The guys who bring nothing but their A-game to work every damn day—stay focused like a laser that can cut through granite, give up all personal distractions, and shut the fuck up about it. These are the guys who deserve the payoffs. Be it Wall Street knighthood or don't-hate-on-me bonuses. It's fair. It's how you play it.

Muay Thai has become my go-to de-stress routine. I work with the Maybach of kickboxing instructors in Manhattan. One hour with him is such intensely gruelling work it cleanses eight hours of workday stress straight out of my pores. It's also a brain spa. You're ticking the whole time: lightning fast, hyper alert. No room for anything but survival.

My right hand is up defending my face, I'm firing my left hand forward—extend, pivot my arm, strike, and pull it back to my chest. Now imagine doing this at blurringly high speed and imagine doing it a hundred times without a single pause. That's one exercise. One. There are nine more to go. The deal is to move, strike, and stand with your weight entirely on the balls of your feet. Not for one nanosecond do you get to rest on your heels. Unless you want to get a practiced uppercut smashing through your face. It's not a threat—my instructor lands it every single time I have the temerity to forget. No matter how much it hurts, how good you get at everything else, he doesn't intend to rescind this rule. This threat. This punishing reminder to be vigilant. This quest to master the moment.

I love the pressure. I thrive on the risk. It's what makes me me. It's a fact. It's a mantra. "I am, first and last, a survivor," I tell Seat 7B. But to her, for some reason, it's so far on the spectrum of her normal, she can't see where I'm coming from.

"I find it odd whenever someone makes this declaration with pride. What does it even mean?"

This is standard operating procedure. I say something, anything—obscure, neutral, insignificant—and it takes on the scale of a presidential debate. Neither of us wants to blink. Since Anderson Cooper isn't available to moderate, our debates remain unending. Unresolved. To be continued.

What does it mean to be a survivor? Duh. "You should know. You threw Nicholas Taleb at me a few hours ago. I don't read him—the guy believes everything he says is a wake-up call for Wall Street that's supposed to ring louder than all the church bells in New York. Not sure about the rest of his grousing, but I go with his idea of antifragile. You don't break under pressure, you just get stronger."

There. We should be done. Dusted. Headsets on and lose oneself in the joys of a classic Hollywood heist film. Or in her case, go back to thinking of shamans and psychic healers or wherever it is her new age-y mind roams.

"So, how's someone who claims to be a survivor different from the rest of us? If you're living then you are getting curveballs your way. That's what the universe does. Not like we have a choice. We survive heartbreak, we survive sickness, losing people, losing homes, losing jobs, losing chances, losing our way—at the end of the day, we're all standing. Leaning on someone till we get stronger, a little out of breath perhaps, but we are standing. To be here is to survive. By declaring we are survivors, what are we hoping to do? Cushion the inevitable blows?"

This has to be a unique skill. Totally unproductive. But a skill, nonetheless. She can take a word and turn it into an entire Aaron Sorkin show.

"Being a survivor is not about surviving like a war-weary amputee. You come out and find the energy and courage to go on, all guns blazing. Bigger and better than before, going after what you wanted—not giving up. Turning into a paranoid wuss is not being a survivor. See the difference?" No. It's never that simple. With her it's about tangential tight-rope walking. Sentimental detours. A dissertation on how love is the answer.

"All guns blazing? Not a wuss? So absolutely no points for quiet fortitude. We must be peacocks of machismo— kick the door open and announce our return like the cowboys in the good old spaghetti westerns—or else we don't get the Survivor medal?"

There's a scenic route and then there's losing your way and ending up in a cul-de-sac in the wrong side of town. Her conversations are the latter.

"Let me ask you something," she says. "What's braver— covering the wounds, ignoring the scar tissue, and braving on, or pausing to acknowledge the pain?"

Anyone who keeps raking up the past is not a survivor. You survived. You're good to go.

"Don't your happy memories give you something? Optimism? Courage?" she wants to know.

So, chronicling the past is the magic bullet for happiness. Where are we, La La Land?

"Am just saying acknowledging pain is like a road map

that tells you what hurts, what helps to recover from the hurt. Mostly, it reminds you that you will recover."

Nah. That's a road map to hell. I'd never use it to go anywhere. I'd rather be sitting in an expensive rooftop bar sampling smoked gin cocktails instead of going over how the man who contributed to my DNA watched his wife toss me out of his home.

I just don't understand why I never told her that. Instead, I told her something I've never told anyone. I told her that sometimes you just need to forget that you can't remember a single day when you felt like a kid after the age of nine. My mother was the only one who made a game out of everything. After she went missing, I kept telling myself it had to be a game. She'd be back any minute. She'd laugh that unstoppable laugh of hers and tell me she'd won and that that gave her lifetime rights to tickle me. Turns out it wasn't a game. Actually, it depends on how you look at it. It's a one-sided game with no rules. She goes away without warning. My already uncool dad turns into an uncommunicative prick. He thinks we're better off without an unstable, unfaithful woman. He never talks about her again. Ever. It's like she never existed. Then he brings a replacement mother who just happens to think I'm yesterday's trash——a foul-smelling nuisance that needs to be recycled. So the game now is passing the parcel. I'm sent to Dad's much older brother and his wife, who run a dingy motel two hundred miles south of Toronto——an oasis of tasteless nothingness. You'd think a childless couple would delight in their new gift of a fully-formed twelve-year-old ready to play. But they were tired and bewildered with life. They couldn't decide if I was the gift that would re-energize them or a burdensome responsibility that would weigh them down. I was neither. I was just free labour—quick, reliable, and smart. Eventually, they were relieved to have me around, as one might be after acquiring the new model of an efficient vacuum cleaner.

"So much for relying on happy memories."

An overlooked, and perhaps the only, perk of having a baby is being able to stare at its sleeping face when you realize you don't have all the answers. Or someone's just interrupted your positivity monologue with a real life example. She pushes a stray strand of hair off her son's forehead and looks up.

"You must have had friends? You're smart, am sure you enjoyed school? Prom? Celebrated festivals? Dog?"

"No dogs. My uncle was allergic to everything—acute asthma—and if he wasn't, he pretended to be. Festivals were a blur of joyless non-events. School was about acing it and taking on more APs than humanly possible. I wanted that college scholarship more than life itself. Prom? The corsage would have bust my annual pocket money budget."

She is quiet. I am embarrassed. TMI. Way too much information! Off the charts. I had mastered the art of shutting the fuck up. What just happened?

She reaches across, hand outstretched. It takes me a moment to realize she is offering me her hand. So I put out mine. We shake hands. Nice and formal.

"You are a survivor. You really are."

Muay Thai has this staggering combination. Switch kick, switch hook. It's a sure shot knockout. This feels like that. Except, I'm not sure who delivered it. Who won?

Or did we, impossibly, land on the same side for once?

Movie Night Wednesday

Azaan has a holiday tomorrow. He was invited for a sleepover birthday party, which he decided to skip in favour of arranging a movie night at home, with me. I'm proud of the off-the-cuff creative programming on his part, but if only it had come before I acted like an obsessive Internet forager trying to hunt down Slinky the Dog (a bit player in *Toy Story*) pyjamas for him.

It began two weeks ago when Azaan fished out the invite from his backpack and declared his intention to attend the party with superhero resolve. Only, he didn't want any superhero pyjamas to do the job in. It had to be Slinky. While I Google-stalked Slinky, I withstood the constant taunting of Spiderman, Iron Man, Superman, and the rest of their super ilk in the form of pyjamas, clothing, entire party paraphernalia—via mocking, in-the-face pop-up ads. I was duly proud of my son's eclectic, non-pedestrian, iconoclastic taste, while secretly wishing he'd conform, just this one time. I mean what's wrong with Spidey PJs? They're right here, one click and $14 away. Who doesn't want to imagine themselves once-bitten-forever-careening across rooftops? Not Azaan. I must drastically cut down the number of times I employ sentences like 'you don't have to be cool like them, you can just be cool like you' when speaking to my boy.

And then on Day Seven, the God of Sidekick Characters descended from heaven and I spotted them. Slinky with his solid front and hindquarters, that famously stretchable metal spring middle (the raison d'être for his name), vinyl ears, and green collar, stretched all around the back of the pyjama top to appear magically and supremely happy-faced in front on the chest. I could almost hear the toy dachshund's gravelled Southern accent calling out, "Don't wait, lady, hit buy, now!" And so I did. When it arrived, Azaan took one look and announced he wanted to wear it every night and day—but thanks to the nanny's unmatched inefficiency, she can never turn around laundry fast enough for us to wear anything again in under a week. Sometimes two.

Anyway, here we are now, Azaan in Slinky the Dog PJs, me—after making a lame-polite-apologetic-last-minute excuse to the birthday boy's mother—and Azad after an entirely uncalled-for apocalyptic meltdown about going to bed, sifting through our movie choices for the night. Oh and there's also Groucho, using up more space on the larger, more comfortable family-room sofa than a family of four.

Riz is in DC on work. I had a write-up to finish. Easily done if we'd stuck to Plan A—Azaan at the sleepover, Azad in bed an hour ago, me listening to smooth jazz and writing a brilliant, moving piece on the astounding human bond between the baby elephant and its mother. But to use an overused mantra of our (business) times: it's time to pivot and embrace Plan B. Toss popcorn in the microwave and get set to watch *Finding Nemo* for the twenty-seventh time, and remain secure in the knowledge that they will not be building a monument of me at the Jane Goodall Institute any time soon. Also, no Pulitzers for profoundly insightful writing in the field of environmental journalism. If anything, I might receive a crippling attack of guilt for missing this deadline.

Don't get me wrong. I love *Finding Nemo*. It's an all-time classic. The Dr Spock of movies. I can lose myself in the hypnotic beauty of the very real underwater world created by world-class animators. But even more than that, I can lose myself in the very real neurosis of a parent played out brilliantly by Marlin, the over-protective clownfish dad. I get it. Nemo is a curious little clownfish kid born with an undersized fin; Marlin is an obsessive parent, worried for his safety. It gets me every single time. No matter how invincible our children might seem from the outside, we always manage to see their undersized fins. Obsess about them. Overcompensate for them. Camouflage their inadequacies, even if there are none! Case in point: despite the inconvenience of being hurtled into Plan B and worrying about why Azaan seems so averse to sleepovers, it's all outweighed by the undeniable relief of knowing that at the end of the evening, he'll be safe and secure, curled up in his Slinky night suit, sleeping in his bed (or mine!), close enough for me to hear his occasional purr of a snore.

"I cannot remember sleeping with anyone until I got to college and then I couldn't wait to sleep with everyone."

You can always count on the inflammatory perspective of Seat 7A on the gentler matters in life.

In the interest of furthering communication, assuming one wants to do that with him, there is only one way to go. Employ the craft of a skilful hurdler working through the obstacles he plants in the form of statements reverberating with bravado and shock value. All you have to do is make room for what's behind them. It's not about the women he slept with during and after college. It's about missing what never was before that.

"A few years ago, the paediatrician frowned disapprovingly after hearing we allow our son to sleep with us whenever he wants to. It was the look of blame and sympathy one might accord the mother of a sociopath."

Oh, this is right up his street. He thinks I'm condoning his bombastic statement and conceding to the fact that I have inept, impractical ideas of parenting. He's practically levitating from his seat with the force of I-told-you-so satisfaction.

"A few weeks later in his clinic, I see pamphlets based on an important Harvard study that extols the virtues of co-sleeping with your children! A laundry list of benefits. It builds confidence, makes them secure, no separation anxiety, reduces stress, creates a stronger bond . . ."

He's not sure where this is going. "Nah, that sounds counter-intuitive. Did you ask the paediatrician what he thought?"

"Didn't need to. Just changed him for someone less judgemental and more respectful of personal choices."

"Sleepovers or climbing into your parents' bed, it's six of one and half a dozen of the other, lose-lose any way you look at it."

I am certain there is a little boy lurking behind that always slightly raised bespoke nose, wondering if a parenting conversation is likely to land him in another maelstrom of opposing views. While unravelling carefully stowed away life stories. Bringing on unintended disclosure. So the urgent need to snuff it out with practiced indifference before it gets too close to the bone.

"I'm not a big fan of sleepovers myself, but you must have had friends you wanted to have endless playtime with, unsupervised time to dream and do crazy stuff with?"

There's no quick-fire sarcastic reply followed by a sardonic smile. He drums his neatly manicured fingers on his tray table and says nothing. I'm about to get back to my TV screen when he says, "New Glasgow was such a dump, my aunt's brother, the only adult I could vaguely relate to, always said you're better off without friends in this place."

The statement is veiled in impossible cool. So cool, you can almost miss the sliver of vulnerability lurking in the shadows of the sentence. He talks about how he was too busy working either to get straight As or towards earning pocket money—from paper routes to carrying bags at his uncle's motel—there was no place for friends. He was way too busy contemplating his escape plans.

"I did have one friend, Jason Chen. He was as desperate to get out of our dump as I was. Jason's family had moved from Shenzhen, but their heads were still stuck in provincial China. His parents were the guys who believed there weren't seven deadly sins, there were eight. Fun topped that list. Jason was the robot who was expected to excel in everything from academics to choir; breaching the contract simply meant committing hara-kiri at the end of the school year. Okay, I exaggerate, but you get the picture. We often discussed who had it worse, on most days it was Jay. Fortunately, my aunt and uncle were too old to employ the energy his parents did on suffocating him with their demands. Being ignored is so much more liberating."

"I think there are immense benefits to a free-range childhood." I have no idea where that came from. I'm always caught on the back foot when we aren't going down a spreadsheet of his dizzying achievements and braggy buying power. Look at it from my point of view. Twelve hours of an unfairly good-looking strutting peacock, oozing self-belief and making no attempt to curtail his obvious disdain of anyone who is not rich, famous, and ragingly ambitious, can change you forever. My gloves are off, my brain never stops ticking for the next comeback, and mentally I am in some form of martial arts crane pose alert—fully prepared to block the next offensive. So when he makes these unexpected admissions of being so human—I'm just blindsided into saying space-filler nothings.

He smiles. "You mean fucked up childhood?"

"Semantics." I tell him. Where did this conversation start? Oh yeah. "Well, at least growing up you had a friend who felt the same thing as you. Where's he now?"

"Jay ended up in New York as well. He was looking for a change; we work in the same place now. He's done well. Got a shit break. Has an autistic kid."

I can't think of anything to say.

"Jay. Probably the only guy who's worth looking out for."

Definitely can't think of anything to say.

"Why does anyone need looking out for? Why?" he asks, like he's asking himself.

I can finally think of something to say. "Isn't looking out for each other the whole point? A mandatory part of our existence?"

"The only thing mandatory about existence is to look out for yourself." He's about to give me a life-changing nugget, I can sense those words powered by testosterone coming my way. "Be unfuckwithable."

Save the World Wednesday

When you're in the business of crude oil trading, head-swivelling salaries that could corrupt Mother Teresa are a given. But there's something sweeter which actually tops the monetary rewards and rarely gets talked about: the receipt of unexpected gift horses, in the form of ridiculous perks, from brokers expressing their gratitude for booking trades with them. On a sliding scale of one through ten, the perks are a clean nine.

Here's a random sampling:

Super Bowl. Front row seats, of course. National football not your thing? No problem, pass on the tickets, make someone an indebted slave for life.

A weekend spent with the premier absinthe maker in California—tasting the louche, mysterious spirit is only a small part of an entire week of drowning in mind-blowing sensory experiences. Wine tasting is so last decade.

Singapore Formula 1 GP. We're not just talking best seats in the house. We're not even going to talk about the pre-race partying with the biggest acts in the music business. Let's talk about the fact that it's a night race through the streets of a crazy perfect city. It comes with lights and glitz and sometimes with dangerous rain and unbearable humidity. It's my sport. *Fast and Furious*—only in real time. Name another sport where billions of dollars are spent to find fractions of a second? And the risk! It's all about the risk. Death looming at every turn. Not your thing? Well then, here's Plan B: watch the race from the thirty-sixth floor in a harbour-facing luxury suite in one of the world's finest hotels. Not even kidding, it's all a part of the subtle 'thank you' package from our broker bros.

Beyoncé fan? Or not. But here's the thing, when you get two tickets to the Formation concert at the Rose Bowl with passes for the after-party, chances are you're already channelling your inner fanboy without having to dig too deep.

It's like glancing at a menu and being able to choose anything or everything. Without ever worrying about the right side of the menu. Or even booking a table. It's done. Picked. Served. Paid.

The montage in the movies? The one where a hit song plays and a string of everything good or sad happens? Right, so this is the montage where you move from one aspirational event to the next, cherry-picking your play time options. It's nothing. But it's everything. Unless, of course, you happen to be Seat 7B, then you'll look at it as some sort of Ponzi scheme.

"So then this is legal?" she asks.

It falls under a broker's client budget. It's business. It's smart business practice. "Of course it's legal . . . ish. I mean, that way you can make anything not okay."

She has this way of looking. Just looking. Not saying. Simply looking at you with the cumulative power of two hundred-and-fifty unanswered (irrelevant) accusatory questions.

"What? So you don't approve of people having fun now?"

She'll blink slowly, like this is a very difficult question involving quantum physics. Like she's juggling equations that the genius of John Forbes Nash would find hard to solve. Like the answer is so searing, so urgent, so important that it has to save the world.

"There's this person, Justin Guariglia, he has a wavy line tattooed on his right arm. Actually, it's a graph charting the average temperature of the earth's surface over the last one hundred thirty-six years. And on the left arm, a similar line reflects four hundred-thousand years of carbon dioxide levels in the earth's atmosphere."

That's inspirational (also a bit nuts). Thank you. But what in fuck's name does this have to do with anything I've just said? This is what I mean when I say she is so random it makes me wonder if she's even all there. Makes me worry for the peacefully sleeping toddler on her lap. Makes me think I could have spent the last ten hours talking to someone more numb than a frozen margarita.

"Good to know. So tell me, does he like Formula 1 racing?" Maybe sarcasm will coerce her lost brain to focus and return from its meaningless wondering.

"I think it's lovely that you people can do all this and enjoy it. But—"

"No, let me stop you right there. Are you implying you'd walk away from the chance to enjoy the good things in life that most people would willingly cast away a limb for?"

"Well. We all enjoy the good things. Yours might be the Super Bowl front row seats. Mine might be a year in Florence. Right off the bat I can tell you it's not happening, not in the next fifteen years." She laughs the half-snort laugh.

"Why not? If that's what you want, go for it. Make it happen."

"Yeah. Don't have the life or the bank balance for that dream right now. But, it's lovely to keep little corners in your heart for the unimaginable."

She's left the building, again. Lost somewhere. Probably admiring Michelangelo's *David* in Florence. By the way, Florence did nothing for me. I'd take Rome. Even Milan.

"So the guy with the tattoo, I don't expect everyone to stop having their idea of fun, but if your tribe has that kind of fuck you money as your tattoo says, then you have a loudspeaker in your hands . . . it allows you to be in places and be heard . . . If we could use that to bring a bit of awareness about the fact that we need to stop saying fuck you to climate change, it would be fantastic."

How did we travel from the joys of unreal perks to Florence to the man with the crazy tattoos and using some fuck you money to bring awareness about the fact that the ice caps are melting? Oh, I get it. Next time, just junk the legendary Super Bowl half-time performance by the likes of Madonna and Justin Timberlake, and instead, get traders to stand with loudspeakers asking people to toss pennies into the stadium to save the world. Perfect. Logical. Practical. This is a wonderful WTF moment.

"Here's a thought. Let's all become hippies, share lofts, and save the world."

"Nah. That wouldn't work. We have to remain who we are and just do a little bit, be a little creative, and raise awareness in whatever way we can, to ensure the earth is liveable for a little bit longer—it's a good legacy to leave."

I want to say she's the activist stereotype: who looks like she might choke if she hasn't vented, lectured, converted or hashtag-shamed the wrongdoers in the last eight minutes. But she's not. I'm not sure what she is. She's never one of anything. Not for too long, anyway. She's incoherent with excitement when she describes a jalebi, as passionate as Frida Kahlo when she talks about coffee, which, let me remind you, she does not drink, she gets lost when she talks about jet trails and mix CDs, she looks teary when she talks about a hug from a stranger, and she talks like a deluded person about saving the world. Go figure.

I could pretend I am getting this shit. Look deeply morose and tell her I'll disembark and go plant a tree first thing. Nah.

"Legacy? I don't know. I'm a here and now kinda guy. Love my life now. I could be gone next Wednesday."

"There's this guy called Dioum, an environmentalist. He says in the end we will conserve only what we love and love only what we learn about."

She tilts her head (again) and looks at me for a while (again). "I hope you'll still be around for many more Wednesdays. Because something tells me you're a good learner."

She takes a moment to blink, or is it to think?

"And the world could do with good learners."

Dash Wednesday

"That's like hoping the Pope will promote Eminem's lyrics," Max tells José and crashes his hopes of getting an outlandish—super creative according to him—funding proposal through. He manages to look defiant and bruised at the same time.

"Come on, Max, it's not the same thing. I'm talking about having roadshows at Little League baseball camps. Captive and involved parents."

Max looks up, suddenly in doubt. "Eminem? He's still a thing, right? Obscenities and angst and repetition passing for music?"

I assure her he is the real thing, but there are lots of them now. There's also his Punjabi counterpart whose obscenities-angst-repetition reverberates through our home all day these days.

She shakes her head. "Rappers. Aren't they all just really angry? Why? Maybe because the guy who had to show up with the melody got drunk or stoned and forgot to show up?"

Axel decides to weigh in, how can he not with his proud German lineage? "Brahms, Beethoven, Strauss, Bach, they would be dying again in their graves!"

Our Wednesday status meeting is supposedly an important one, mandatory attendance, and one that ensures everyone's on the same page. Or, as much as an eclectic, passionate, disorganized, greater good-chasing, absent-minded group of people can hope to be. Now someone's talking about Nicky Minaj, and not because she's got anything to do with any of the projects on hand. Because she knows how to rap, I'm told.

Never ceases to surprise me how music has the power to bring people together and the power to send people in dramatically diverse directions. Riz. An old school music aficionado, known to fearlessly strum and sing *Stairway to Heaven* after six beers, is a diehard believer in the unrivalled transformative powers of a curated mix CD. The act of choosing, sequencing, and creating the list is an art, not science, he claims. He'd be appalled if you thought it was all down to technology. The fact that today we can seamlessly share an iTunes playlist with the click of a button only strengthens his argument of going old school—making that enormously personalized effort. "It's an act of pure love," he likes to say. "You're actually giving and revealing a part of yourself to the receiver." Having said that, I can't remember the last time Riz actually did that. A mix CD curated for a romantic reason! What I can remember is the first time.

"The mix CD and why I got it remains one of the most defining moments of my life." He looks genuinely perplexed, this man who believes oversized diamonds and meals that cost more than the GDP of small countries are the only acceptable form of romantic gestures. How could a curated CD, being handed over to you by a guy about to get on a plane to travel a gazillion miles away, be something that defines anything? Stevie Wonder did put it into succinct poetry, 'With the right song you either forget everything or you remember everything.' Seat 7A says he can't think of a single song that has the power to change anything. I tell him I feel like the same song can change us again and again.

Riz visited India every other year to spend time with his grandmother who lived next door to us—we shared a common wall. Not exactly like the one a certain misguided leader of the free world wants to build between the Mexican border and the United States. This was more of an apology, less of a wall. Barely four feet high, it was way too comfortable to be even mildly daunting to discourage trespassers. In fact, it was inviting, almost begging, to be sat on for purposes of perusing the world go by on a summer evening. Baba and I often sat on the wall and looked up at the sky. Except by the time I met Riz, he was gone and I really didn't like sitting on the wall anymore. Standing against it was acceptable. Or sitting with your back against the wall and reading on a winter afternoon was almost enjoyable.

"It was one of those evenings that everyone has lived

through. All your friends, their friends, everyone you know distantly and barely know, even your sociopath cousin—every single person is invited to a party. I can't remember why I was the only person under the age of twenty who was home and pretending to enjoy it.

"I could hear the plucking of guitar strings and faint humming from the other side of the wall."

"Why do you even remember an underwhelming day like that?" Seat 7A is supremely amused, flashing those dazzling white teeth that belong in an orthodontist's pamphlet.

"It was the day I met the guy who was going to be my husband."

"What's that got to do with music or being the girl who was never invited to sit at the cool table?"

Always reassuring to know the man without a detectable smidgen of sensitivity is never more than one silly comment away. There's no need to tell him Riz was strumming 'Stand By Me' on his guitar. It was a strum-slap sort of arrangement, remarkably effective—soft, but never off-key, and then he started singing along . . . a few lines and then the chorus . . . *So darlin' darlin' stand by me*. It was possibly the combination of an exceptionally beautiful October night and the overpowering smell of frangipani in our garden or the fact that I was uninvited to attend anything anywhere . . . I remember leaning against the common wall and being acutely aware that I was caught in a profoundly beautiful moment. And I could sense the possibility of something even more extraordinary about to unfold in the next one.

The thing about Seat 7A is this. When he's completely engaged and wants you to go on, he does it by pretending that listening to you is his burdensome civic duty. A pretence so transparent, it's come to feel almost endearing.

"I had my back to the wall and something made me want to turn and look across, see the face behind the voice. I knew, I just knew, if I did, nothing was ever going to be the same again."

I pause because I realize I am sharing a deeply personal moment with a complete stranger, which, going by recent evidence, he isn't likely to understand or appreciate. It's hard to ignore the fact that he's sitting very still, like he's really waiting for me to go on. Why let precedent come in the way of a good story?

"When I turned around, this guy across the wall looked up, but he didn't stop playing or singing—it wasn't loud, in fact it was pretty soft, but I could distinctly hear the words. *So darlin' darlin' stand by me.*"

Blank face. No response. I can actually hear the second hand ticking on his expensive watch. He finally speaks. "And so that's exactly what you did, stood by him."

"Well, that was the general intention, but it took a lot longer. Riz lived in Ohio, I lived in Delhi and was only halfway through college, so we did the good old-fashioned thing of long distance. Instant Messaging saved us."

"Wow, you've been married that long? Before FaceTime calls were a thing?"

He's the kind of un-cerebral, unintentional funny that makes you want to laugh or mock him or maybe even knock yourself cold for engaging with him. He's fascinated with the idea of long distance on the strength of Instant Messenger. He can't stop asking about it.

"Two years of only messaging? Are you serious? And this must have been pre-emoji. Wow, that's serious hardship right there."

Actually, it was oddly eloquent. We said so much. Felt so inseparably close. So achingly far. "That was when I discovered my favourite sign."

"Seriously? You have a favourite sign—let me guess, the less than sign followed by the number three?"

Despite dating my marriage to the Bronze Age, he seems to have put me down as a giddy Japanese adolescent girl of today. "The dash."

"The dash? Like that little line in a sentence?" He's doing it again, trying to sound derisive when he's actually curious.

"Actually, it's what makes the sentence."

"Erm . . . reminder, words make a sentence"

"That's the thing, place a dash and it takes away the need for words. Consider this, there's a dash between the two most important dates."

He raises a quizzical eyebrow.

"Between the year you're born and the year you're gone. So, the dash is life itself. It's about feeling everything. Here and now. It looks like a simple line. But it's like this intake of breath . . . the perfect pause . . ."

Why do I feel like he's holding his breath? "It's also hope, because there's always more to come after a dash."

I can tell he's trying to search for a slicing, witty piece of sarcasm, but instead he surprises me with a genuine question. "So how do you respond to a dash?"

"By knowing that you, in this moment, are everything."

Black Wednesday

It starts off as just another Wednesday. Unless you're Seat 7B. Because then my previous statement will be rendered instantly inaccurate. There's no putting Wednesdays in a 'just another day' line-up. She believes all days are not born equal, some days are more equal than others: Wednesdays come with a halo. She believes nothing bad can happen on a Wednesday.

"I had Thursdays off in school when I was growing up. So Wednesdays became extra special. In my head, I still hide the rule book on Wednesdays. We may eat breakfast for dinner or ice cream for starters. It's lovely to toss it up in the middle of the week for no reason at all, isn't it?"

Batshit crazy is what it is. Like her view on most things, real or obscure. Like places are not worth visiting for what makes them famous. Getting to the top of the Eiffel Tower and having a meal at an exquisite, unaffordable restaurant is inauthentic. "Big occasions, landmark places, milestones are never the stuff of real memories. Life lives in the little moments in between. The cup of tea you make for someone just because it's about to rain." Yes, please go write that book on hippie-romance on a micro-budget while I enjoy a thirty-year-old single malt as an après in my favourite landmark ski-resort.

Track back. Tuesday was sitcom-scene perfect. Drink with the city's top headhunter wooing me for a killer job at a derivatives trading firm. The sort of firm that's oozing Godzilla buying power and offering the moon made from blemish-free De Beers solitaires. Undeniable ego boost. But not bait worthy enough for me to jump ship. Just seeing what's on offer was enough to grow from my standard five foot eleven inches frame to six foot two inches as I shook hands, said thank you but no thank you, and walked tall out of the bar. It was a Sunday morning feeling already. So I didn't join my team for a night out to celebrate George's birthday and a whopper week of trading. Instead, I went home and stayed with the Sunday cheer in my veins and watched *Love Actually*, again. This often much-maligned holiday classic is my go-to staple for a perfect wind-down evening at home. So yeah, it's British saccharine, bursting with romantic clichés and celebrity actors. Sentimental sap! But it works. Like a restaurant view of the Eiffel Tower amidst a billion lights at night always works (you listening, Seat 7B?). Like Colin Firth's urbane, sophisticated writer falling for a Portuguese, non-English speaking domestic helper works. Like real life never works. So quit the intellectualizing and sing along with Bill Nighy's washed up, self-loathing rock star—Love is all around.

Because then you wake up the next morning—Wednesday—feeling like you can't wait to take the day on. Alarm at 0430 hours. Five-mile run. Egg whites, whole wheat toast, black coffee, and out of the door by 0630 hours.

So, I am at my desk, my day sailing along en pointe, when it takes an unexpected nosedive. Turns into a minefield. Markets plummet lower than Lehman's assets the day they filed for bankruptcy. More bloodshed in eighty minutes than in an entire season of *Game of Thrones*. Everyone was juggling with swords on their trading desks.

If we had it bad, Jason was incarcerated even before the markets started to tumble. An oil refinery in Italy exploded, sending a devastating cloud of gas across Europe and wreaking havoc on Jason's trades. It was a double whammy of unprecedented scale. The perfectly controlled air-conditioning wasn't helping. He was sweating like he was in an overheated sauna. Larry psycho-yelled for him. When Jay left Larry's room, it was like he'd left behind all powers of cognitive recognition: he slipped out of the office without his bag, his phone, or a word.

That night Natasha came in from Paris for a meeting. She decided to stay an extra day. Two nights with Natasha, and yet Jay was on my mind the whole time. I tried calling, but he didn't answer his phone. Of course, he'd left it on his desk. He'd left all his things on his desk. I wonder if I should clean-up for him—save him the embarrassment of coming back. That might imply he should be embarrassed about coming back. He shouldn't be. A massacre on the trading floor on a bad day can end your job. It doesn't end your career. He needs to come back and walk out with his head held high. The man has been a star performer for twenty-two months straight.

Three days go by. Most of us are back in the saddle, cautious but optimistically working our way back from the carnage. My book is looking reasonably good. Jason's desk is like a still life of the fateful day. Everything is exactly as he left it. A vivid reminder of the chaos and trauma he'd lived through. Nobody talks about him. It's like he was never there.

I step out for coffee but drive to Jason's apartment instead. Juglio, the doorman, tells me the family is on vacation. How can that be? I call Amy, Jay's wife. She's at her mother's place in Boston with their son. She hasn't spoken to Jay for two days. I keep ringing the apartment. Knock incessantly at the door. Wait in the lobby. It's time for all the generous tips over the years to pay off, I decide, and convince Juglio to use the spare key to open the door.

Jay isn't around. I exhale. Start to breathe a little easy— why the heck was I so tense? I walk around the apartment, everything is in place. Jay has to be fine and probably on his way to Boston. I am about to leave when I decide to pop into his bedroom. There he is, sleeping peacefully. With his shoes on? And his tie? Then I see the small mountain of white powder on his nightstand.

Up close, he doesn't look like he's sleeping peacefully. "Jay! Wake up!" I'm yelling. For some reason, Juglio is staring at me. Like I'm the problem. I grab Jay's arm. It's ice-cold and minus the faintest trace of a pulse. I keep telling him to wake up—that's all I keep saying: urgently, loudly, stupidly. Until Juglio puts his hand on my shoulder and says, "I'm going to call 911."

Never Say No Wednesday

"We know that a sea turtle can live up to eighty years, some even live until they are two hundred. Now take one guess how long plastic lives?"

Some tentative voices wager a guess. "Forty years?" says a cute little girl with a ponytail. A little boy bursting with bravado takes a wild guess. "Three hundred and seventy-seven!"

"Close enough. Only, it's even more. Plastic is a stubborn, stubborn substance, it can live for five hundred years. So here's what happens, every plastic bottle, every bit of plastic you use is somewhere, in some form, floating around the planet."

Sure, they're only elementary school kids, but keep in mind they're going to be evaluating The Paris Agreement someday and I'll bet anything, they'll be doing a far better job than our generation.

RECYCLING RUNNERS is a massive school programme that gets school kids involved in the business of consciously recycling at school and eventually in their homes. Today, we just happen to be at Azaan's school. He looks shy-proud to see all eyes on me. It must be odd to see all the kids around him hanging on to every word his mother says. The same mother who at home is just someone who rushes around to change his brother's diapers, keeps his nanny from over grooving, turns into Cruella de Vil when his dog climbs on the black sofa and sheds enough golden hair to weave a six by four rug, urges him to eat his cereal as fast as he can— not so fast . . . *hurry*—four minutes before the school bus arrives!

It's that awkward age where there's a twenty per cent chance he may race towards me and almost knock me over with a high impact hug involving all his limbs and most of his head. Then remain marsupially snuggled for another whole minute or more. Odds are, he's much more likely to stand at a distance, lift a tentative hand, and execute a covert half-wave that he hopes the kids around him will miss. He may turn around and leave with his friends to go play a game he doesn't really love but wants to be a part of for the sheer pleasure of being a legit member of the group. As a parent, I drastically underestimate this innocent shift in behaviour. I slalom between relief (yes, he has friends!) and aching acutely for the unsurpassable joy of a spontaneous public hug that never ends.

A group of industrious second graders have surrounded José and me with a buffet of ingenious recycling ideas. They call themselves the Nature Ninjas. I want to spend the whole day hugging these glorious warriors. Only, I'm staggering under the weight of my fifty-three-point job list moving in my head like the lead pair in a Latin dance competition. We have a family of four, whom we have never ever met and are barely related to, arriving from India and staying with us for the next five days. All because Riz found it hard to enunciate one simple word: No. It's like the world would descend into chaos and impenetrable darkness if Riz were to ever employ the use of that fairly normal, commonplace, yet hugely effective word. I'm not much better either and that's exactly the problem! There's no bad cop. There's good cop (him) and then there's pushover cop (me). Why couldn't we just tell them this was a massively busy work week for both of us, and Azaan has a school project, and Azad has an immunization shot, and the nanny is threatening to take a day off to view another prospective suitor, and we have only one spare bedroom and they are four adults, and . . . I could list two million reasons for us to say a soft, gentle, but firm no. Instead, "Yes, of course! It's absolutely no problem," was what Riz said. Telling his grandmother's brother that we're happy, no *delirious*, to take care of these barely-related relatives.

When he hung up, he looked like he was about to start a petition with change.org to save this family we'd never met. "They're on their way to Ohio, apparently on a crazy small budget. Lost their little cloth store in Lucknow to a fire last year . . ." Of course, now I feel like a bitch.

The guilt gets me, every single time. Seat 7A's face

flashes before my eyes: I can see his fingers placing air quotes around the word 'guilt' in the sentence "And you have guilt going for you." I can also see him looking preposterously cool, striding down Wall Street and laughing at me as I contemplate dinner options for our house guests who are partial to desi food (translation: all four meals must be wholly constituted of Indian food). Riz says he's got this (translation: he's given Karim Bhai, the jolly Pakistani owner of the dive round the corner, a heads-up to be on call 24x7). Bet Seat 7A calls his favourite celebrity chef to do the honours when he has one house guest for one day.

Well, at least we're done at the school meet. José is handing out special gifts to the kids who call themselves the Composting Crew. I get behind the wheel and try not to think of Seat 7A's ridiculous, not even remotely funny joke. "What's the name of the new Tom Cruise eco-thriller?" Frankly, I had no idea Cruise was starring in an eco-thriller, but trust Mr Movie Mad to know this. Also, Cruise fancies saving the world, so why not? Except, he's not. The joke's on me. "Mission Compostable!" Seat 7A announces, beaming with little boy one-upmanship. So much for scalpel-sharp wit.

Two hours later, I feel like I've let myself into a stranger's home. Eight bags of varying sizes are lined up in the living room, there's food everywhere (clearly, Karim Bhai, of the eponymous Karim's, has relocated his headquarters to our home), and complete strangers are jaywalking through the premises as if on an unguided tour of a famous landmark location. Riz smiles at me as he emerges from Azaan's room, arms full of stuffed toys and Azaan's favourite blankie. "Hey, thought it might be fun if Azaan officially moves in with us this week."

We finally escape to our bedroom and I look at Riz for a really long time. "This cannot be extended beyond five days. Please learn to say the word."

He smiles as he places Slinky by our bedside. "Yes. Yes. I mean yes, I am going to say no. Definitely." He lingers, as if he's trying to remember something important. "They said they are happy to even sleep in the living room . . . No, no, I know that's not your thing! But poor guys, they said they are extremely informal."

I stare at him dead serious and he keeps smiling like this is all very funny. "But I am not informal." I say this without any trace of humour. On any given day, Riz has the most disarming, open smile in the room—any room, anywhere. Not today. I'm just really annoyed today. He finally gets it. "I'm not doing this for more than five days, Riz."

"What have you done with my wife? Please bring her back."

I'm unable to smile. Complete humour deficit. I see his smile, but I don't see it.

"She's taking a time-out. She needs it," is all I can muster up.

He nods. He gets it. But he's Riz, you see.

"Listen. Let's slip out of the fire escape. We can do this. I've convinced Ms Yo Yo, she's staying over for the next five days."

"No wait, where's she going to sleep?"

"They'll figure it out. Come, let's run."

I would. Only, I'm so exhausted I could sleep for a week.

It's All Her
Fault Wednesday

The aftermath of Black Wednesday devolved into an underwhelming routine of the usual (wins) at work. With one major difference: the complete absence of thrill. Also completely absent was the joy before the hunt, and those jet-propelled streams of high-pressure endorphins that went coursing through the veins after the kill.

For large chunks of the day I feel nothing. Absolutely nothing. Then without warning, I'm standing on the frontlines, in the line of fire: my head, the target of an efficient, unsolicited, multi-pronged attack. I'm dodging high-calibre bullets and grenades with pins pulled out—thoughts that I don't want to feel or know how to ward off. There's this one question, a sniper's bullet, which never fails to make it through all the barriers I've built: what could I have done? I want to believe the answer is absolutely nothing. Clearly, it's the wrong answer—the question never stops hitting me. With perfectly timed mechanical repetition.

I thrive in order. Order has always been more effective than I imagine any therapist can be. My sense of order urges my head to type up my thoughts into a perfect alphabetized list, then reorganize the list in descending order of importance. It flashes in and out of my head, a never-ending PowerPoint.

Blitzkrieged.

Disbelief. Not Jason. He would never do this. Never.

Guilt. I didn't see it coming. I didn't have his back. Why wasn't I there to pick him up after he bottomed out? Clean up after him? Send him to rehab?

Disappointment. Why is everyone at work acting like Jay never existed? He's been wiped clean from his desk, the conversation, our collective history—he's not even being brandished like an example of what not to do, which might have been less demeaning. It's like there was no Jay. He was a guy who gave two years of his life to this place. He was a seriously valuable asset. A friend . . . fuck it, our family.

Anger. There's a lot of stuff to be angry about. But mostly, I'm just mad at Seat 7B. How does she just make up shit? And how the fuck does she say this shit with such conviction? Nothing bad happens on a Wednesday. She said that. More times than I care to remember. Can we all have what she's smoking? Just cover the hard facts in her totally unrealistic schmaltziness, maybe then I'll never have to wake up in a cold sweat telling Jay you don't get to quit!

What did she do to become this way? Go to fairy-fuckin'-tale finishing school?

I treat my head like a canvas, keeping it blank for as long as I can. Until without the slightest warning, it gets splattered incessantly with a riot of paint that drips in all directions—a regular Jackson Pollock. I once attended the opening of a Pollock retrospective at the MOMA. Not because I care about art, but only because the invitees included Anna Wintour, Jamie Dimon, Donna Karan, Jerry Seinfeld . . . Basically anybody who was, is, will be, anybody in New York. There was so much talk about his iconoclastic drip paint style. To me, the paint-splattered canvases looked chaotic and the product of drug-fuelled anger and confusion. Honestly, I'm one of the few guys on the team who doesn't have my dealer on speed dial. I haven't had many adventures or misadventures with Quaaludes, meth, or crack cocaine, but the way Seat 7B's thoughts keep splattering across my mind, it feels like I have to be on some form of good quality hallucinogen.

"You bet. Losing someone is always unfair."

". . . acknowledging pain is like a road map that tells you what hurts . . . It reminds you that even if you're lost, you will find your way back. . . . Mostly it reminds you that you will recover."

"I love fall. I just love it. There is no better example of impermanence and the startling beauty of loss."

It is fall. And there is no startling beauty in losing anything. Or anyone. Note for you, 7B, stop gathering leaves from under the sycamore tree—leave that to the movies—just get with the programme. People are not burnt orange leaves falling in slow motion, people are not startling beauty when they fall. They are hopeless, dead, cold, leaving behind a gaping hole and a big fat mess for their families.

She's back with the unswattable zeal of a telemarketer determined to sell you a credit card you don't need. "Did you ever play the trust-fall game as a child?"

No, I didn't. Not as a child. Nor as an adult in some stupid corporate team-building exercise. It's counter-intuitive. There are no king's horses or king's men waiting to put anyone back together again. "The game is to be the last man standing."

"The game is to learn to let go. To trust your friends. To know someone you love will catch you when you fall."

What's the best advice to give someone who lives inside a Hallmark greeting card? Every sentence you utter needs to stop sounding like it's composed of stardust, pixie dust, fairy dust, angel dust, and fennel effing pollen. "You don't get to do what I do and go falling over backwards hoping someone is going to catch you—recipe for breaking your back and inviting people to walk all over you."

"Wow. You know what, they should just replace the Charging Bull statue in the financial district with a monument of you. The true symbol of strength, charging on, never falling."

There you go. She wants to romanticize everything . . . even falling. Make falling a team sport.

Today, instead of offering me the usual highs, the kinetic traders at their desks, the noise, the clamour, the hunger, the tension, the fear, and the euphoria only serve to exempt me from my surroundings. I feel an epic bone-tiredness seeping into me. I step outside for some air. A few minutes later I find myself at Attilio's. Why does his espresso taste like distilled cardboard? I sit at an empty table, zoning out, unable to focus on anything. Other than the fact that I wish I could take a return ticket to that flight that day and tell her what I think of her hashtag bliss, naïve, logic-free zone of existence.

I realize Attilio's been talking to me. "So your friend—she never come. I look always. But nobody like her."

You bet. Nobody like her. Annoying as fuck. A terminal migraine. An obstinate picketer who has taken over every inch of my head.

"Sometimes, if somebody stay in your head, it is because they supposed to be there. There is reason."

For fuck's sake, Attilio? You're going to start talking like her now?

Fall Wednesday

Azaan is an incessant fallen leaf collector. Fall is the time of year he and his imagination are in overdrive. It also sparks off long philosophical discussions on the circle of life. Not to mention rapid-fire questions, mostly concerning the well-being of fallen leaves. "Does it hurt the leaves when the colour changes?" "Is the tree the mama who is losing her babies?" "Are they going away forever?" "Are they died?" Yes, died, not to be confused with colour change or dyeing. That's a whole different discussion.

Homeless people, the short lifespan of butterflies, the weak parenting skills of the panda mother (and this is why I aggressively unsubscribe to the affectionate moniker of Panda Mom), the tragedy of a sparrow with an injured wing, a flashing television image of a hurricane-hit home in a far-flung place, the sudden knowledge that a friend has a single parent—just some of the things that turn into rapidly spreading stubborn rashes, constantly pulsing and itching Azaan, which won't go away without the balm of lugubrious discussions and unending reassurances. Sometimes I feel like I want to guzzle the abominable drink of the season, a spiced pumpkin latte, use its million calories and sickening sugar intake to fortify myself with the requisite energy to take on his angst-filled questions of the day.

To be honest, I'm never sure if he brings home fall leaves because of their ephemeral beauty or because he feels sorry for them from imagining their separation anxiety. While the other kids are happily-crazed Ninjas crunching over heaps of dry leaves in the park, Azaan is mostly looking to spot and rescue a still un-crunched leaf. How do you not love a kid like that? Statutory warning: sometimes you're going to find yourself wishing he'd straighten those curved-down worry brows and join his buddies as they laugh with uncontrolled child-villain glee—kicking, stamping, and bringing on a dry leaf blizzard like it's a rite of fall passage.

In Seat 7A's parenting book (a voluminous one, written with the hubris of those usually not yet parents), Azaan's worrying, sensitive soul is entirely the outcome of my wishy-washy ideas. It was a harmless funny story. Provoked by a conversation about the silly things we do to protect the people we love. Worst executive decision of my life to think someone who barely knows me, has never seen my older son, or how I choose to parent him, is an avid proponent of the theory which states the less children we have the more we profit, would be the person to share this harmless, funny story with. And yet I did.

On Azaan's fourth birthday, he asked for a single goldfish. Not a pair. Not an aquarium with fake rubber plants and obstacles passing off as deep-sea decor. Not a confused ecosphere populated with exotic-coloured brag-worthy sea creatures. Just one goldfish in a large clear bowl. Simple enough. Only, it ended up feeling like Riz and I had been selected to be a part of NASA's recent airborne mission, designed to save Australia's Great Barrier Reef. The said bowl had to contain just the right amount of purified, temperature-controlled water and a filter so efficient and expensive it might as well be used to clean up the Hoover Dam. Finally, when it was all set up, a single orange goldfish, in her carefully curated space-age pool, was swimming back and forth with enough ascetic grace, ease, and tireless repetition to put Michael Phelps out of business. The effect was marvellously minimalist and entirely mesmerizing. Azaan spent every waking hour with his face pressed against the bowl, whispering his best-kept secrets to the goldfish he'd chosen to christen 'Sushi'. Which, I must admit, I found mildly unsettling, but Riz clapped his hands in spontaneous approval and called it Roald Dahl-like ingenuity. Despite paying more for the bowl and its accoutrements than we could recall paying for any piece of crystal we still didn't own, we ran into a few unexpected problems. I returned one morning from dropping Azaan to school to find Sushi Phelps floating lifelessly in her bowl. I figured I had two options: one, use this as an opportunity to explain the circle of life and quietly flush Sushi down the pot, or two, ignore the elephant in the room, or the dead fish if we want to be hobbled by semantics, by quickly disposing of Sushi's body and replacing it with an identical live fish before Azaan gets back from school.

"Who wouldn't pick option two? Naturally, right? Except, I became a repeat offender. The fish replacement operation went on for six weeks! Each week, with monastic precision, and creepy repetition, the newest Sushi would breathe her last and I'd be racing to the Aqua Pet Store for a replica.

"Until the day I got the timing of my weekly heist routine just a bit off, and there he was! Azaan, peering into an empty bowl, with nothing but perfect symmetrical bubbles being pumped to the surface with quiet efficiency. He just stood there—like he'd actually walked into a real Roald Dahl story—stupefied. I felt like an evil criminal mastermind.

"I had no choice but to have the talk. I tried telling him Sushi had gotten sick. He had a perfectly logical query: had I taken her to the animal hospital? I knew in his head he was seeing his goldfish being resuscitated, probably by a many-armed octopus surgeon using his prowess and his handy limbs to fix Sushi and send her home at the earliest."

Seat 7A cut in, "Tell me already you stopped covering up and just let him know that shit happens."

"Those were not the exact words I used. But we did go for closure. I lied blatantly and informed him that Sushi had been given a small, sweet burial. There were some tears,

Azaan said a prayer, then resolutely announced he'd prefer a clownfish next time."

"So eventually, he did have to deal with death—you could have saved yourself weeks of craziness."

"Well, the weeks of craziness, as you call it, is a fond and funny family memory that I hope to recount in detail to Azaan and his kids someday. As for his dealing with death or hurt, sure, everyone has to, but if I can soften the blow for someone I love, I'll pick that option. Every single time."

I can sense a sarcastic comeback heading my way and then it changes its course. Swapped midway for a look. Empathy? Then he looks away. Perfect. Make me feel like a supermarket trolley with recalcitrant wheels, the one you walk away from because steering it in the right direction is never worth the effort.

Time to Come Home Wednesday

Larry looks human, but I'm certain he's from a different species. Or, as an infant, he was dropped on his head. Repeatedly. He lives on the fine line between homicidal megalomania and mind-fucking generosity.

Two weeks after Black Wednesday and Jason's passing, he declared an impromptu celebration was in order to acknowledge our comeback, a bumper trading day at the office. "Fuel for your efforts, boys!" His assistant arrived with a carton of Larry's favourite wine du jour, Balthazar Château Margaux 2009 (only $3000 a pop), accompanied by a delivery guy toppling under the weight of multiple boxes of Larry's favourite pizza from Nino's Bellissima (arguably the most expensive pizza in the world)—topped with three types of caviar and sprinkled with Maine lobster ($820 for a twelve-incher).

The quantities bordered on ancient Roman gluttony. We were just sixteen of us. Used to be seventeen. Jason was missing.

I had visited Jason's wife two days ago. She was unsettlingly composed, holding their son's hand, offering me coffee, talking about the medical examiner's report like we were discussing a newly released movie. It took all my willpower to stand there and not run out of the door or just stand there and not throw up. It turns out the time of death wasn't Wednesday night, after all. It was Thursday, 2.10 am. I'm still not done being mad at Seat 7B. It wasn't a Wednesday, I'll give her that, but that doesn't take away from the fact that she's still full of lame bumper sticker lines and she still keeps slipping in and out of conversations without warning and without being invited. Without being here!

The wine and pizza, meanwhile, were a big hit. Why wouldn't they be? You're hungry as fuck after a frenetic day of trading. Unexpected Michelin star-quality snacking is better than sex at this time. There was also the perfect accompaniment: industrial quantities of backslapping and self-congratulating. I couldn't even look at the pizza without working up unwanted bile through my digestive track and I certainly didn't feel inclined to give up still water for that ape-shittingly expensive wine. Not out of guilt. Just out of something that was wrong. Something uncool. Something stupid. It felt like a badly timed ridiculous cliché, like a back to front Yankees cap at a tuxedo event. Mostly, it felt disrespectful to Jason.

Here's my take: every single guy sipping that $3000 wine deserved to be beamed up (or down?) into bro purgatory, led by Larry and his aggressive showmanship. It felt like I was seeing him for the first time for what he was: a swaggering bully who gets away with pervasive, unrepentant exploitation because of the carefully cultivated I'm-a-genius-so-I'll-do-anything aura and his sudden bursts of irrational generosity. Let's get real, it's the nature of the beast, it's what we do and the shitloads we get in return. Unfortunately, it neutralizes all his psychotic behaviour. Until you begin to ask how can it be okay to sidestep and walk around the guy who's on the floor? Funny co-incidence, Jason really isn't there, everyone's just sidestepping around the imaginary chalk outline of where his memory should have been.

I'm holding invites to the opening of a new rooftop club in the city. Apparently, the invitation includes a helicopter pick-up for two, which lands you on the helipad from where you're escorted inside the club. Natasha isn't around. But more importantly, I don't think my head is around. I toss the invites into the bin, knowing full well that most people will gladly part with a couple of high functioning limbs in exchange for these. I haven't quite put my finger on why I didn't pass these on to someone. Anyone. Maybe it's because I can't seem to fight the feeling of being stuck in a party I can't wait to leave.

If there's an opposite of a carpe diem moment, mine's got to be this. Remember *Southpaw*? Jake Gyllenhaal's battered and bruised pugilist, Billy Hope, who loses everything and tries to get back up—in life, more than in the ring? Before he finds his philosophical, melancholic mentor in Forest Whitaker, he has his shark manager (played by the iconic 50 Cent) remind him, 'Billy, you know if it makes money, it makes sense.'

Of course it does. Except on some days it just doesn't. And on those days you remember someone who makes more sense. We were talking about the dream dinner party list. One person who featured prominently on Seat 7B's list was Roger Federer. She had this fanatical admiration for the guy.

"Yeah, yeah, we all know he's a legend, but come on, he's kinda over the hill and a bit of a crybaby. I can name twenty other sports heroes who deserve my undying adulation," I remember telling her. She looked at me as if I was personally responsible for nailing Jesus to the cross.

"It's beyond sports. He's a life lesson. In a time when we see nothing but chest thumping conceit, drug-enhanced sporting accomplishment, sell-outs, and victories without a modicum of grace, he stands on the side of art and accomplishment without ever sacrificing decency."

"Whoa! He's not running for president. We don't need a character endorsement . . . we need killer instincts and stamina."

"For twenty years he's decimated his opponents on the court, but he's never disrespected them. He honours the sport every single time he steps on the court. It's like he's in constant meditation, only, he's moving with the speed and lightness of the wind."

This is a woman in love. In love with decency, way more than she is with the sportsperson for his sporting prowess.

"He has nineteen grand slam titles and more prize money than most countries have in their reserves, but it's never about that. So if he sheds tears of happiness, of victory, of defeat, he's paying his respects to a game he raises and releases like art, like Michelangelo who said, 'I saw the angel in the marble and carved until I set him free.' There is nobody else like him. You know, I pray there is someone by the time my sons grow up . . . someone who is an example of inhuman skills and a stellar example of humanity. He proves you can be both."

I'm about to remind her he comes from a privileged background and was a bratty teenager . . . something to bring her celestial hero down a notch or two. Before I can, she smiles with lit up eyes. "They should test his DNA, he's definitely not entirely human . . . he doesn't even have sweat glands."

Decency? I see one of the boys scrape and scoop a spoonful of caviar off his pizza slice, pop it into his mouth, and wink at me. I feel like suggesting to him he should choke himself with his lanyard when he's done wolfing down the caviar.

Tony Yan Tak, one of the best-known Asian food chefs in the world, claims he never got into cooking because of any great love for food. He did it for the money—the love followed the money. A lot of his signature surprise dishes reflect his love for wealth and then food. Including the humble fortune cookie. It's never what you think it is. There's no sage prescience printed on sketchy paper when you crack it open. Instead, there's luscious caviar or expensive truffles or a tiny scoop of Tahitian vanilla bean ice cream and specks of Amedei Porcelana. The first time Jason and I ate there was when we'd gotten our first salary cheques. After we paid for the meal, we had just about enough to cover our rent. Unforgettable meal. We felt like sultans of a country as we walked out of the restaurant. It's seriously weird to think I'll never ever walk out of a ridiculously expensive restaurant with Jason again. Or laugh senselessly from an overdose of rice wine when our careers depended on behaving with decorum. Or joke that we escaped our hellhole neighbourhood in Toronto and our certifiably insane families. All you had to do was survive one bad trading week, Jay. One bad trading week, dude!

I call Natasha. She's with a client. She wants to know if it's urgent. I tell her it's super urgent. I can see her excusing herself and stepping out of her client's office—a picture of poise and control. "What's up, babe?"

I'm finding it hard to speak. To swallow, even. But I know exactly what I want to say. I don't need to look for the words. They are waiting to come out.

"It's time to come home, baby."

There's a long pause.

"Listen, I know you're upset about Jason. And I'm so sorry, babe. This is the worst thing ever. But it's not the end of the world. You're going to get through this, you're such a fighter. Such a survivor."

"You really need to come home, Nat."

"Look, can we talk about this later? I'm in the middle of—"

"No. We're always in the middle. In the middle of something. We need to be together."

"Are you asking me to stop doing what I'm doing? Give this up? Leave Paris? Come there and do what?"

"Be here. Be together."

"I'd never ask you to do that."

"Why don't you?"

"You're being unreasonable."

"It's time to come home. Will you?"

"Do we have to do this now?"

I'd be deaf if I didn't hear her answer.

"I guess that's a no."

Gangsta Wednesday

Azad's familiarization at his new school provided all the proof we needed to confirm that the gangsta, the tyrant, and the charmer is born, not created. Also, theories of nature vs nurture were entirely debunked in the forty-five minutes we spent watching him interact with his future educators. It was hard to tell if his teachers and teachers' assistants were shocked, delighted, bewildered, or even equipped to take on the task of educating a two-year-old with a bafflingly odd mind of his own.

Azad's best friend is Zachary—Argentine mother, English father, Scottish au pair. Our nanny gets along famously with the au pair— perhaps they exchange notes on Yo Yo's dubious lyrics and the mysteries of why haggis is allowed to be called food. Somewhere along the way, Azad acquired a Che Guevara Basque-style beret (Argentine mum's fangirl influence?), complete with authentic-ish silver metal star in front, and a fondness for the word 'splendid' said with aplomb and a real Scottish slant. I felt vaguely guilty for not having a miniature Nehru cap handy for Azad to pass on to Zach. Neither did I have a handy Hindi buzz-worthy word to share, but on that score I could rest easy as our nanny had taken it upon herself to teach Zach the lyrics of a masterfully age-inappropriate song called 'Dope Shope'.

Azad wore his revolutionary headgear and strutted into school, sans any trace of nervousness or Azaan's legendary clammy hands or the slightest hesitation to behave like our family owns the school. When asked by the principal, "How are you feeling today, Azad?", he placed both hands in his pockets and replied "Splendid!" We knew we could dispense with the socialization formality right there and give Azad more time to do his real job: topple regimes or assist Jeff Bezos in expanding his empire. Instead, the principal asked him, "So what do you like to do?" I wish he had hesitated for a fraction of a second, looked like he may consider saying something on the lines of 'Playing with Lego bricks or watching *Madagascar*' (which he does at least three times a week, by the way), but he did neither—he didn't hesitate or come up with a predictable response, instead, he said, "Rapping and eating." I could swear the principal cast a surreptitious glance towards the parking lot—like she was half-expecting a tour bus exploding with groupies waiting for their rock star to join them. I heard loud laughter, it wasn't the principal, it was Riz. Of course. The principal smiled the obligatory we-love-chutzpah (but maybe this is too much) smile and went for her third question. "And what do you like to eat?"

"*Dhokla.*"

I feel like it needs to be said—Azad's had dhokla maybe twice in his entire life. Honestly. Where was this even coming from? How could a two-year-old be a spin doctor?

The last question was to do with fun. Azad told them he liked to pee on the dog. It had happened *once*! The nanny had decided to let the kids bathe Groucho for fun. But the water had stopped for a moment and while she was looking into it, Azad decided peeing on Groucho would help get the shampoo out of his eyes. I didn't even try to explain to the hopelessly shocked principal this was not a daily activity in our home.

Back on the flight, Seat 7A had watched Azad wake up intermittently, gobble down food, take an energetic waddle down the aisle, cast a stoic glance at his fellow passengers, and then spread out on my seat like he was the crowned monarch of the airplane.

"He's going to run for office or certainly run a company… And it sounds like your other one will be catching fireflies to lighten the electricity burden on the world."

I can't decide if it is another instance of his malignant narcissism (like he's the consummate expert on all things from child psychology to career prophecies) or it is just a harmless joke.

Either way, it slides me right back into banal point-scoring mode. I start scoping through my brain to recall this priceless article I had recently read a hilarious takedown of guys exactly like him. Guys who actually live life by the formula: Great mind + incredible body = winningness to the power of awesome. I so want to repeat verbatim, every scathing, ridiculing line from that piece.

"Someone wrote this perfect piece about you. I think it went: every day I wake up at 3 am, which is half an hour after I go to bed, and scream, 'I'm crushing today!' For breakfast, I snort three raw eggs blended with the tears of my competitors and that's when the hustling starts. I hustle twenty-six hours. Of course, I am in peak physical condition . . ."

I will give him this, he gets that the joke is on him. He says, "Go on, this could really be me—"

"So I run constantly, even when I'm sleeping. I could be a marathon world champ, but I'm too busy smashing it being a business role model. But when I go to the gym, it's me versus the equipment. I do not stop till one of us breaks. I've destroyed six treadmills."

"I think I get the picture," he says, laughing.

It strikes me then, that ever so rarely, arguments and harmless insults can play out like comfort food. Easing the opening of doors into conversations you may hesitate to have with friends, but somehow, not with strangers.

"I take it you always knew you'd be noble and altruistic and adopt the material needs of a hobo?" he asks.

"Actually, I didn't."

"So you wanted to be an investment banker?" he asks with a grin in his eyes.

"I wanted to be an astronomer."

"So why didn't you?"

"Two reasons. I wanted it for pseudo-scientific reasons. Actually, zero scientific reasons, only romantic reasons— the stars, the sky, the moon, and my father—who wasn't an astronomer either. And then there was Mom. Strong and decisive and selfless and noble. It felt almost wrong not to learn and follow."

"No pressure, huh?"

Riz is giving me a ride to work after the school interview. "You called him Azad, were you expecting anything but a free spirit?"

"Free spirit, yeah. Tsar, hunter, trapper, rapper, Sicilian crime family head, used-car salesman, Jay Z's natural heir— no."

Riz is laughing so hard, he can barely keep his hands on the wheel. I'm certain we're going to career off the road. And then our little mafioso would have to look after his gentle, sensitive older sibling for the rest of his life. No doubt, to the background score of some awful Punjabi rap.

"Much as I hate to admit it, maybe Seat 7A made a valid prediction about Azad."

Riz looks confused. "Who?"

"Remember the guy on the flight, helped me with the diaper change?"

"Oh yeah. The show-me-the-money, shallow, annoying, braggy man-child?"

"Yeah . . . Okay, maybe I was a bit harsh. He could be funny and sensitive when he wasn't trying too hard."

Riz turns to look at me. "Yeah?"

We're almost there. Riz says, "Why don't you call him over for a drink or something?"

"Are you kidding? You planning on buying a Central Park-facing penthouse anytime soon?"

We pull up outside the office. "Hmm. Prospect Park to Central Park . . . At the rate my start-up is growing, we might have to lean on Azad to pull off a bank heist or wait another ten years."

I'm about to get off the car. "I'll wait."

"So you want what he's having before you can make friends with him?"

That's such an odd, un-Riz thing to say.

"Maybe he does have a terrific work-ambition-success ethic, but it's not for me . . . us . . . so, no, I don't want what he's having."

Riz smiles, reaches over, and gives me a kiss before I get off the car.

"Good. This is us. But I think we can still be friends, with anyone, even the plane guy."

Something tells me we can never be. We are simply destined to bump into each other's thoughts—sparring partners at best—engaged in a never-ending imaginary battle. Or maybe, thinking back and (very rarely) seeing some sense in a ridiculously opposing point of view. Proof that sometimes one meeting can last a lifetime.

Marathon Wednesday

'When you are backed against the wall, break the goddamn thing down.' My friend Harvey Specter said that about taking a no-win situation and making it your win. I said that when I chose to sign up for the New York City Marathon. It was never going to be the I-can-but-maybe-I-can't tentative half marathon. It had to be the whole 26.2 miles. They say distance is your only opponent, the killer, the destroyer. I say, bring it on.

Natasha moved out last week. Technically, she never moved out. She didn't have the bandwidth (hate that word, it's code for you/ the task at hand are just not important enough) to fly out from Paris and remove her personal effects from my apartment, so her dad rented the services of an elite packing concierge. The sort of guys who carry enough tissue paper to give Seat 7B nightmares and prompt Al Gore to kill himself by diving into a melted Arctic ice cap pool in horror and shock. The painstaking finesse employed in packing each and every piece of her clothing, shoes, bags, made me wonder if they were full-time employees from the luxury department of Bergdof Goodman. Six hours later, I had more walk-in closet and bedroom space than I'd had in two years. In fact, it felt empty. Although, I have a fully furnished designed-to-perfection apartment. And way too many clothes in the closet. So maybe I felt empty.

I don't do empty. I fill up empty. With purpose. With plans. With repeat viewings of movies that fit me like a pair of lambskin leather gloves with cashmere lining. I work harder and I workout even harder. Only, I don't feel inclined to do the former anymore. Work had a gaping hole the size of Jason. Jason was a compact-ish Asian-American. So that's not a Kobe Bryant-sized hole, but it was exacerbated by the fact that everyone at work was starting to seem like a self-absorbed prick.

I did workout harder. Upped the Muay Thai frequency and routine. Started running longer and harder. Note to self: constantly play back piece of graffiti read outside a bar on the Lower East Side: *You're allowed five emotional minutes in the day and then you gotta be gangsta.*

Running
Work
Muay Thai
Client dinners

Broker engagement parties
Two very cool dates after the parties
Running
Cryo Spa
Running
Headhunter meetings (I'm considering a switch to one of
the Big 3 consulting firms. Yeah I know, the perks and the
pay will be a step down, but I'll live.)
Running
Nutritionist visit: recommended meals for marathon
Running. Running. Running.

Checking all the boxes.

That's a packed day/week/month/life—every slot
accounted for. There really was no space for anything.
Except, large, massive chunks of this:

Blank. Empty. Nothing.

There's always stuff in the margins though. All those
scribbled words—all invisible. Words that return like unpaid
EMIs. Thanks to Seat 7B.

"You think I do guilt? I think you do safe." She'll announce just out of nowhere.

"Illuminating insight. But in case you haven't been listening, my entire career depends on my ability to take risks."

"Maybe that's why for everything else you do safe? It's a massive liability, letting people in. So you build these impenetrable walls."

"And you would know this because you have an advanced degree in psychotherapy. No wait, you have Internet access."

This time she doesn't look like she's waiting to drop a tactical drone in response. She looks at me and says nothing for a really long while, like the discussion is over. Then says something that goes on to become another annotation that hovers in the margins of my empty page. "Letting people in isn't just inconvenient, it's white-knuckled high-risk stuff. And frankly, the stakes are too high. Someone with your risk evaluating abilities would see that, it's a no-brainer. Shutting them out makes complete sense. Until that moment when you feel like you're so isolated on the inside, you want to break down the wall, every single brick, so someone can see you. Actually *see* you—bruises, bumps, bad haircuts, and inexplicable aches. Every carefully curated and covered up thing. But then no one can get in."

I think I may have revived my role of the privileged jerk at that point. "Did I tell you one of our many perks at work is access to a leading psychiatrist who happens to be a star performance coach? I know you believe huggers replace therapists, but also, FYI, it's just so much easier to tap in on a $500-an-hour professional or better still, do what works best—remain unfuckwithable."

"You would know. You're this big winner at the game of life—money, perks, smart girlfriend—destiny achieved."

"Hell, yeah! That is the meat on the plate. The rest of it is bean sprouts and tofu. But it's the meat that builds your muscles."

She starts laughing. "That is the worst analogy ever!" She finally stops that snort-laugh of hers to ask, "So I'm the tofu in your metaphor?"

"Well, since you always look at me with an expression of acute intestinal distress, I think it makes perfect sense, actually."

This time she has a longer laughing fit. "It's not you—"

"Oh, I think it is me and it's my type, all the evil-doers in the world, your world."

"Look, we'll never have anything in common except our dramatically opposing but honest views of the world and our place in it."

"Exactly. So you bring lots of . . . what did you call it . . . empathy and hugs and deep quotations, but newsflash: the world needs jobs, wealth generation, spending, growth, and I'm proudly Team Capitalist."

"In keeping with my lost child, bohemian, deep quotes image, I have only one thing to say, hashtag slow clap."

Okay, so that was funny.

I'm on my second espresso at Attilio's. He thinks me looking at a job change is a 'Fantastico idea'. He's wiping down his already pristine white espresso cups like it's a compulsive therapeutic exercise. "You know, my mama always say happiness come before success. Not the other way round."

Kill me. This is playing out like a hostage drama. The only two people I speak to (well, technically, I speak to one in person and the other one in my head) are life guru-ing the shit out of me. I can never escape.

Or maybe I can. Marathon training is seventy per cent mental, and thirty per cent physical. You teach your mind to handle it and your body follows. The training is the marathon. You hit impenetrable walls and you work your way through them. You train your mind to finish that race or die trying. I've got no time for empty pages. Seat 7B is just going to have to make a permanent exit. No more notes in the margins. No living in my head. No subtle putdowns. No more sound bites from her tired repertoire of played out quotes and insights into human understanding learned from her kids' storybooks.

I prefer lessons from life. And the movies, of course. Friendship—you have it right there in *Fast and Furious 7*. Vin and Paul's characters. Paul died just before the movie came out. That tribute to Paul at the end was the best thing a friend could do. Made grown men cry. It still does. That whole untimely death and your friend gone, in a heartbeat. Not some dark secret of paralyzing shame that one cries. Each and every time that song comes on.

It's been a long day without you, my friend
And I'll tell you all about it when I see you again
We've come a long way from where we began
Oh, I'll tell you all about it when I see you again.

RIP Jason.

'Tis the Season
Wednesday

We say this every time the year comes to a close and it isn't going to stop me from saying it again. With heartfelt incredulity: where did the year go?

It's already November. Again. It's boomeranged right back! We'll barely get through Thanksgiving and we'll plunge into Christmas. The crowds, the last-minute gift shopping frenzy, the rampant consumerism—none of it can put a dampener on my spirits. The holiday decorations, the shopfront windows (Macy's, Saks Fifth Avenue, Barney's, Bergdorf Goodman, Bloomingdale's!), the skaters at Rockefeller Center and that giant Christmas tree (clichés to some, beloved perennials to me), the skinny Santa at the corner of the street from our office, the artisanal Christmas markets that spring up overnight and provoke you to sip apple cider even if you hate apple cider—a moving, living, pop-up holiday greeting card, love it all. Okay, I may have overstated my case just a tad. I love it all, with the minor exception of parent participation in hyped up pre-holiday activity at school.

Who doesn't know the US Army recruiting poster that depicts a passive-aggressive accusing Uncle Sam pointing his finger at the viewer: how dare you not enlist in the war effort? Now replace Uncle Sam with Aunty School Mom. I fear she stares at me from everywhere—billboards, buses, kiosks, magazine covers, my deepest slumber, and real life. Azaan decided his interest in nativity plays was over. Let the records reflect I had nothing to do with his decision (does auto suggestion count?). I sighed in relief and moved back to the business of putting together a forty-page write-up on the joys of partnering with Disney to teach children their first ideas of sustainability. Imagine the beauty of combining Disney stories (*Frozen*?) with melting ice caps. Max, José, and I were drunk on the idea—maybe even figuratively. We were at Max's place—she was nursing a sprained ankle, we were all nursing glasses of Prosecco—appreciating my work on the Disney document noticeably more with each sip. While Max's avocado-loving partner was serving up photo-worthy small bites, admittedly most of them had lots of, a little, or a hint of avocado. But it was all so perfect. Exactly like the season. That's when I got the call.

Uncle Sam's finger was a maladroit apology in comparison to Aunty School Mom's accusing tone. "Azaan says he doesn't have a sheep outfit? Today is a full costume and props rehearsal, this is most inconvenient for us." So it turns out Azaan had a change of heart, Riz signed 'some form' he thinks, and Azaan is now playing the sterling role of a sheep in the nativity play, mostly hidden by baby Jesus's crib, if I understand correctly. A part that could be played with remarkable ease by a giant wad of cotton wool. "These grown-up, *Mean Girls*, narcissistic, Type-A control freaks who make butting into school business more important than breathing, deserve a nuclear missile up their busybody asses." Max's calm, mature, and sagacious observations were the exact morale booster I needed to banish all thoughts of abandoning our session to go hunting for expensive costumes in sheep's clothing—through the deathly swarm of peak traffic. Also, it wasn't my fault that the PTA had, without warning (or was it mentioned in that tediously long email that I had postponed reading?), brought forward the Christmas play by three weeks?

"I think I'm an okay mom, but I think I'm a majestically inept, reluctant, deeply insecure school mom," I confess to Seat 7A during our what's-the-one-thing-you-can-never-get-right Q&A.

"What's a school mom?"

"You're lucky you have to ask! Oh, it stems from the Parent Teacher Association, but goes on and becomes this daily competition to do and outdo and prove and win mom-eat-mom contests to show you're involved in the education of your child. Not for the faint-hearted."

"Sounds exactly like an average workday for me."

How can I not laugh at the lustrously right comparison? That's exactly what it is, a Wall Street primer.

He can be funny, especially when he is deviously trying to avoid the matter of owning up to a weakness. I am not about to let up. Kryptonite time, Superman. "Now, your turn."

"No, hang on. How do you deal with it? Tell me you're not going to opt for homeschooling?" Why does that question sound like it's actually a judgement passed in bold subtext: exactly what a flaky free-spirit like you would resort to?

"I deal with it like I imagine most of us deal with what goes against our grain—slay the annoyers in my head and smile good-naturedly in person."

He's grinning now. I continue, "Actually, there's something else I love to do. I imagine myself lighting and releasing sky lanterns into the air."

Now he's genuinely puzzled. "Why?"

"I love them. Also, in some Asian cultures they believe sky lanterns are symbolic of letting your worries and problems float away. I could watch paper lanterns floating into the sky forever—it has to be the most beautifully soothing sight in the world."

"Even if they aren't made of recycled paper?"

José refills my glass with some more bubbly, an unmasked attempt at ripening the atmosphere for some off-topic talk.

"He could do that. Bring a million floating paper lanterns crashing and burning down to earth with one silly comment."

Max is looking at me over, and not through, her reading glasses. "He's not going away any time soon, is he?"

I could have masqueraded as the innocent. Run the gamut of what-who-are-you-crazy line of deflective questioning instead of answering. Only problem is, Max is a human lie detector.

So I succumb to honesty. "I feel like we have this unfinished business in the form of pending arguments." Max is staring at me, while José looks like the cat that swallowed a bushel of canaries for breakfast, lunch, and dinner. Luckily, José gets a call and drifts away towards the kitchen. Max continues to wear her neo-Nazi interrogation expression.

"He is this princeling of Wall Street, engaged in relentless self-improvement, wealth accumulation, and banishing feelings because feelings are a sign of weakness, and oh, the route to world domination is via ridiculously expensive material choices. Need I say more?"

"Yes." Did I mention I've always suspected Max was trained by MI6?

"As we speak, he's probably hosting a famine for super models or having a crisis over a sartorial emergency."

"And yet, he's in your head more than climate change is in Al Gore's?"

I think shrugging is always the right response; unfortunately, stream of consciousness monologues are my default setting.

"Like I said, it's like this . . . this never-ending argument. We are on two ends of the spectrum—so we'd have these head-on collisions on just about everything."

"But you're the least contentious person alive. It's been about a year. And you've never met him again."

"I know, right? But see that's the thing. Even though he acts like having feelings is the worst, most intractable mistake, I believe he's pretending. I mean, he watches and learns from the movies! He feigns scorn, talks with messianic zeal about the haute life, but then . . . keeps wanting to know about ordinary stuff like the kids' personalities, why I am moved by jet trails . . . and he did volunteer to help change Azad's diaper when I was sick. He walked him up and down the aisle . . . twice."

Max doesn't ask, she just waits for more. She elicits more! It's the interrogator's innate skill of letting the other person fill the silence. "Despite the carefully curated, suave, man of the world, no-damns-to-give irreverence, he has this inner decency and this . . . this inner lostness? It's like he's sending up a flare in the sky, hoping to be rescued."

Max says nothing at all. She sips her wine. Looks at me squarely and sighs.

"Looking back, those fifteen and half hours were like being hermetically sealed in time . . . with a complete stranger who turned out to be anything but a stranger. Of course, we remain strangers. There's no past, no present, no future. Just sealed in time forever."

Until this point I've assiduously avoided allowing myself to think this through, let alone articulate it. The words feel uncomfortably alien out in the open. They also feel profoundly true.

"Now, our conversations, our disagreements, our odd exchanges appear from nowhere, like a printer's smudge on my day. . . . I'm talking back in my head, like he can hear me.

The purpose is simply to win the argument. That's all it's about, really. Winning those on-going arguments."

Max gets up and hobbles around the room. Like she's looking for José and her avocado-obsessed partner. But she's not.

"These are called feelings. Not arguments."

"Arguments? Feelings? Just semantics, right?"

Max sips her wine, but I know that's just a comma before her comeback.

"You don't see this as a pending argument, you see this as some pending past-life connection, and you're worried as fuck."

Grand Central
Wednesday

"It's like entering a grand cathedral. No matter how many times I enter, I just cannot take its splendour for granted. I feel like I've stepped into my favourite page in history—the marble and brass, the majestic staircases, the opulent chandeliers, the arched windows, and the soaring ceilings. To me it is, and shall always remain, the most romantic spot in the city. And that clock! How much time has it seen? Sitting like a monarch on top of that brass pagoda, still regal after more than a century. Everyone's favourite meeting place—how many proposals, teary goodbyes, happy kisses, and heart-wrenching hugs has it witnessed? Did you know Sotheby's has valued the clock at $20 million? I think it's criminally undervalued—it's priceless."

That's WikiShe for you. Seat 7B can put a used-car salesman to shame when she's going on about something she loves. Coffee she doesn't drink, school meetings she hates to attend, Roger Federer's genius, glorifying punctuation marks. Not to forget, the Grand Central Terminal.

I am out on my usual run, supposed to be heading west, when I find myself turning east into 42nd street—like a GPS gone rogue, I begin heading towards the Grand Central Terminal. I enter and find myself staring up at the celestial ceiling, trying to remember what she had said about it. Did she say the mural was actually upside down? There was some big story about the architectural plan being on the ground one way and then being executed on the ceiling another way? Or was it Orion that was upside down? That's the problem with all that passionate detail—overkill—you can't remember anything! Anyway, right now, the main concourse is exceptionally crowded. I stand by the information booth wondering how often she passes through this exact same spot. Does she pass through at all? Will she pass through now? I feel light-headed. Is it the crowds or have I been running too long? I sit on the steps and wait for the feeling to pass.

The light-headedness gives way to an insoluble unease. Or maybe it is something else. Something I cannot put my finger on. Something I can't remember feeling ever before: an overwhelming sense of being alone and no desire to do anything about it, except sit on the steps and wait. Wait for the feeling to pass. It just won't, despite my need to see the last of it, it insists on overstaying—like an unwelcome stock market plunge that flatlines and refuses to surge, despite all the pundits' predictions.

I can't remember how long I have been sitting there. How long I have been waiting. And for whom. When I get up to leave, I realize my cheeks are wet. It is too cold to sweat. How can they be tears! Why would they be tears? I have a party to be at in three hours. A deep tissue massage scheduled before that. A quick drink with my headhunter squeezed in between the two. I want to get up and go, get on with the evening's carefully laid-out plans, but every molecule in my body is protesting like it wants me to wait and watch. All I can watch is the blur of motion: nameless people rushing around me. I try to listen. I can only hear one person: from the mistakes on the ceiling to the wonders of Orion. "It's the show-off constellation, located on the celestial equator and visible throughout the world. Just waiting to be spotted. Although named after a Greek hunter, it should have been named after a Greek showman."

Our conversations have become a punishing fusillade that won't go away. I'm starting to think the only way they will is if she were to walk in right this minute, through her favourite New York City structure—in flesh and blood, oversized sweater, vanity-free loafers, unmade-up—carrying her toddler, and acting like a handy nearby defibrillator that could jump-start my heart: to feel annoyed, amused, insulted, combative. Alive. Those questions. Those ridiculous questions!

"Two words. Which, according to you, are the most important, life-changing, cherished words? I'm not saying three, because then people resort to the cliché. So, two words." She has an arsenal of thinking up stuff that is so not important or useful . . . so completely immature.

"Why don't you tell me, since you've obviously thought this through—you clearly have a lot of time on your hands."

"It's me."

"What? How does that even make sense? Sounds like half a knock-knock joke."

She laughs really hard, then begins one of her impassioned monologues about nothing. "It's me. It's like telling someone you can be you, you can break, you can let down your guard, you can fall, you can falter, you can fail . . . I'm right here. I'll catch you. It says you're home. Mostly, it says, you are loved, no matter what."

Oh, well, that was a dictionary of all my don't-dos right there. Note to self: in that case, never use those two words or succumb to them.

"So what would be yours?"

"It's all about self-preservation, and no two words can get more shit out of your way and let you do exactly what you want to do, get exactly where you want to be, than fuck this."

I'm thinking now that that probably wasn't a titan of a comeback. It was just a dick move. I'm also thinking I'd like to pull out the force majeure clause in our contract of constant crossfire. It feels like unusual circumstance, forces beyond my control. Making performance inadvisable, commercially impracticable, illegal, or impossible.

What I am saying is you are different. Imagining you were ordinary was a miscalculation of historic proportions.

I think if you, Seat 7B, were to walk through the main concourse of your favourite building right now, I'd be happy to walk up to you and call it a truce.

It's Friday not Wednesday

It's long-weekend madness and our home feels like a stadium filled with Vuvuzela-blowing addicts. Just for some perspective, and because I have the luxury of a trivia collector colleague like José on my side, the seemingly harmless plastic contraption and noise weapon of choice for sports fans, can belt it out at a hundred and twenty-seven decibels—louder than a lawnmower (ninety decibels) or a chainsaw (hundred decibels).

Riz grandly offered his brother and wife the option to drop off their three kids (ages five, eight, and nine) to give brother and wife the chance to avail some sort of you've-worked-so-hard gift from work in the form of a week-long trip to Hawaii. Irony could be clad in a grass skirt and dancing the hula, and Riz would be guaranteed to miss it. *We* were overworked, understaffed, and, right this minute, also just a bit overwrought.

Azaan finds his sheep costume too needle-y (itchy, in non-kid parlance), so he has decided he wants to act in the play—the very same play that is to begin four hours from now—in his pyjamas, which have sleeping sheep on them. Also, we decided, imprudently I might add, that we'd bring Christmas forward so the cousins could open their gifts together. Azad asked for boxing gloves for Christmas—I'm just relieved he didn't ask for a Harley Davidson or a pet anaconda. We actually managed to get a pair that might fit him, and then un-divine intervention prevailed. Groucho got to the shopping bag before we could hide its contents in the to-be-packed closet and made a meal out of one glove. Now it has three fingers and a thumb less than it should. We desperately need new toddler boxing gloves.

Breakfast is in progress and feels like a picnic in a sports stadium. Painted faces, Vuvuzela noise levels, some crying, and lots of food. Riz, like a multiple-armed Indian god, stands over the breakfast table refilling glasses with juice and milk, eating, passing, hoisting Azad on his shoulders to make him smile (end goal: make him eat), and asking Google Home: "Hey Google, where do we get boxing gloves for little boys?". In one fell swoop he's just, albeit innocently, debunked the theory that Santa is real. Maybe not for Azad, who seems to be content chewing Riz's hair while comfortably perched on his shoulders, but certainly for the other four. There's an instant torrent of anxious questions regarding Santa's authenticity and whereabouts, which I stoically ignore as I butter toasts and use every ounce of self-control not to toss the Google Home device down the garbage chute.

Nanny is grooving to something—I do not hear music, she does not have on headphones. The only thing playing is the news on the television. As they say of some of the best dancers, she was born with the groove. All hail Yo Yo.

The questions from the kids about Santa's whereabouts, his existence!, are coming at me fast and hard. Feeling like a sleazy lawyer who's found a devious escape clause, I simply hand over the accused: "Daddy?" I must grudgingly grant him a modest percentage of aplomb for spinning a credible and creative take on the Santa gaffe. He tells them how Santa, like everyone else, relies on technology for higher efficiency and better distribution. After contemplating the fate of Rudolph and his ilk, the kids are now gathered around Google Home like they expect the device to beam them up to North Pole, or at the very least, grant them a one-on-one with Santa or a member of his crew. The nine-year-old hovers between cynicism and curiosity while the others are already discussing the possibility of upping their Christmas list.

Riz turns up the television, then turns to me with an odd look on his face. "Some kind of explosion, I think." I keep looking at him, almost hoping to delay looking at the TV screen. I can see the red band screaming BREAKING NEWS, but the volume is too low to hear the what and the where. The news anchor's face is replaced by paramedics running towards what appears to be office buildings. Riz moves closer to the screen, I know he doesn't want the kids to hear or see this. I walk towards him. "Wall Street. Apparently one guy in a truck rammed through pedestrians. Fourteen injured, not sure about the fatalities yet," he says softly so only I can hear him.

I feel a paralysing sense of uneasiness. Riz turns away from the screen, dismayed. "Shit, I think Addy mentioned he was meeting someone there this morning. Let me give him a call." He starts looking for his phone, then looks up at me. "Hey, wasn't your airplane guy on Wall Street?" Before I can respond, Riz is talking to someone on the phone.

Whenever these incidents occur, and they do much too often in the world we now live in, an invisible lever goes down, switching on every searchlight everywhere to singularly focus on race and religion, making them instant minefields of taut emotions. I marvel at Riz's ability to step out of that equation. Maybe he's just made that way or maybe it's the most valuable lesson he can teach his sons, me, the world. A brick of anxiety sits heavily in my stomach, making it hard for me to focus on the tightly packed agenda of the day. I wonder if Seat 7A works close to where it happened. I wonder if he saw any of it. I wonder if he's safe.

"They're saying it was some unhinged guy, throwback from Occupy Wall Street, bring down capitalism kind of loony. The cops chased him down," Riz says and switches off the television as the kids have shifted their attention from Google Santa to us. Age Five is now spinning around like a whirling dervish, while Azad sits on top of Groucho and yells, "Splendid! Splendid! Splendid!"

The knots in my system refuse to loosen up, making breathing a conscious and laboured effort. The news flash has managed to successfully douse out my chronic love for the season and replace it with a million prickly nerves. It feels too close to home. Much too close.

One of my million conversations with Seat 7A begins to play back on cue. I talk about a caring deficit in the world. He talks about the increase of chronic haters who don't want anyone to do well because they're too lazy to do it themselves. "It's hardly that simple," I remember saying. "Actually, it is. If you're always playing the victim card, you become resentful and sometimes you tip over and start demanding, and even doing crazy stuff." Of course, he can reduce the problems of the world into two neat piles—the ceaselessly energetic, successful haves and the malcontent have-nots. "From a posh soiree in a glass-and-metal penthouse it might seem that way, but—"

"Forgive me, I am not a practising saint. I am not going to adopt a Syrian family just because I got a fantastic bonus for busting my ass last year—don't I pay enough in taxes to make the world a better place?"

That's one way to look at it. We should leave it at that. Only, he's not done. "Look, I didn't grow up like Rashid Belhasa."

"Who?"

"Probably the richest fourteen-year-old on the planet. Fun fact: he owns a custom-made Louis Vuitton Ferrari in his fleet of fifteen high-end cars, son of an Emirate multibillionaire, has a cult social media following, runs multiple businesses of his own."

"Your point being?"

"At his age, I was lugging bags and cleaning crappy loos in a dodgy motel, pumping gas, and studying like fuck for seven APs despite never having dropped my GPA below 4.0 through high school, only so I could get a full scholarship to college. Which I did get and still had to work lots of shit jobs to keep going till I graduated and got the job of my dreams. So excuse me for not feeling that if you don't have what I have then I am a tool of Satan."

That's a truly impressive backstory—I genuinely can't decide if he's a triumphant, larger-than-life hero or a doomed one. Either way, I feel for what he's been through. But that wasn't the point of what I had started off saying. "Look, I don't mean you. I mean a rampantly materialistic world which is so visible thanks to social media and technology. It's just making everyone neurotic."

"I'm too busy having a life, so you won't find me on social media."

I feel this urgent need today to ask a question I had no inclination to ask then. "So where will I find you?"

Their Wednesday

The news channels are on an endless loop about the Wall Street attack. It's thrown an immovable dark shroud over the city and effectively squeezed out every last ounce of cheer from the holiday season air. There were two fatalities, as it turns out. Two people who must have woken up, had breakfast with their families, made plans, kissed their loved ones, and talked about meeting later. The comforting, unthreatening, everyday routine of just another workday. And look how that turned out. The gossamer threads of happy lives, wrecked in a split second. All it takes is one unhinged, angry person.

The brick of anxiety that descended into the pit of my stomach when this began hasn't dislodged itself. If anything, it's gotten heavier with every passing day. I've been a high-functioning robot—executing the demands of work, five kids at home, and the general pre-holiday frenzy with model efficiency, sidestepping the heaviness, the recurring bouts of restless uncertainty, and the inability to put my finger on a growing sense of foreboding. Like nothing from this point is ever going to be the same again.

We're swirling in busyness at work—caught up in the well-meaning urgency to get as much as possible wrapped up before Christmas. Nanny brought her cousin over to help with the extra work around the house. For some reason, the 'cousin' looks more Chinese than Punjabi, but I don't think it is my place to question her ethnicity based on her facial features. It helped that Riz reminded me how she had once shocked us with an unsettlingly short haircut that had to have been inspired by Kim Jong-un, so we conclude there must be some Southeast Asian lineage in her Punjabi family. Besides, I feel too preoccupied with something that is starting to feel like mild panic attacks—shortness of breath, inability to focus, and random stabs of dread—since the awful news on Friday. It makes no sense, really. Everyone I know and love is safe, but the uneasiness continues to linger and fester, like a diabetic's wound that doesn't regenerate healthy tissue, doesn't heal.

I am driving uptown for a meeting, scheduled to join Max at three o'clock at the venue. I get there much too early, with thirty-five minutes to spare. Without a moment's hesitation, I know what I have to do to rid myself of this gnawing restlessness. I have to know Seat 7A is safe. I don't have his name, his number, his address, the name of the place he works at. He isn't on any social media, so there is one, just one eyelash of a chance of finding him. I have to find Attilio's and show up for the coffee invitation from a year ago.

"So there's this place on Fullton Street. Attilio. Six tables, small, tiny. Best food. Unbeatable coffee. Once you have an Attilio espresso, you'll kill yourself before having any other coffee. Next Wednesday?" His words play out like he's riding shotgun.

I haven't been this side for a while; it takes me some time to navigate legitimate parking, which is about fifty metres from where I need to be according to Google maps. I'm walking past a Korean grocery store, a hip juice bar, an old-fashioned tobacconist . . . no sign of Attilio. I'm looking at the map, standing below a striped awning when I realize I'm right there—the place is so unobtrusive, the sign so small, I have walked past it twice. This faceless, obscure place? How could this have entered Seat 7A's bragging hall of fame?

It's even smaller on the inside than it appears to be from the outside. Only one of the six tables is occupied—two women in sharp business suits are as deeply engaged in their desserts as they are in their conversation. It feels like they've had a sudden sugar craving during a boring work meeting and slipped away to succumb to the pleasures of an authentic tiramisu. A waiter walks out from behind the coffee bar, carrying two cups of espresso to them. An overwhelmingly rich coffee aroma fills the air, as if all the wood in the place was dipped in espresso before being made into furniture for the specific purpose of coffee-enticing even the most rigid non-drinkers. I find a corner table and settle down.

Now that I am here, the ridiculousness of what I'm doing hits me like a sobering dunk in ice water. I'm here to ensure a stranger I've met just once in my life is safe. I'm here because? I'm here because.

I can just leave before he walks in. If he walks in.

The waiter is standing over me like he expects me to know what I want, minus a menu. "Um, do you have some English tea?" He smiles like I've just finished telling him an un-funny joke. He points to a chalkboard above the coffee bar that has something written with chalk which I honestly can't read minus my distance glasses which I never remember to wear. I'm squinting at the board, when I hear, "Bruno, I help the lady."

A short man, mid-sixties, he could be Mr Miyagi or a Sicilian crime family head—it's hard to decide. He has the kindest eyes though. An Italian Mr Miyagi is what I settle for.

"So *bella*, you don't drink caffè?" I shake my head. "But-ah you like the smell, huh?" What is it about Italian men and their ability to cut through the clutter and speak to your heart whether they are twenty-six or sixty-six? Clearly, this is Attilio.

My phone starts buzzing madly. I glance at it, it's Max. I text her: Delayed. Please don't wait.

When I look up, he is looking at me, just looking at me. It's not creepy at all. It's like he knows me. Which is impossible. "I'm actually looking for someone who comes here a lot . . . I think."

"Yes?"

"He works close by. He says you have the best coffee in all of New York. He—"

"Tall man, good-looking man . . . Indian?"

"Yes, tall, Indian . . ." I'm about to say camera flash smile, but then I realize that's the semi-sarcastic tone I'll use when he walks in, not on this gentle old man.

The man looks away, looks towards the entrance. "Yes, he come every day almost. Two-thirty." Like he's expecting him to walk in any minute. I'm bracing myself for the long, easy strides. The swagger. The insouciant smile. And the fact that he may not recognize me. The good thing is, I can get up right now and leave.

"Oh. He's late? Or did he already come?"

The man shakes his head. "You meet him where?"

"Um . . . on a plane. Just this once, actually."

The man stares at me for an eternity. He lifts his fingers and taps the side of his head. "But-ah he live in here . . . always, huh?"

I don't know what to say.

"One hundred and ninety-five countries, hundreds of islands, seven seas . . . but one stranger, one meeting, and nothing is same again."

Trust Seat 7A to talk about Attilio's coffee and not this. This. This unsettling talent of speaking like a man who sees things no one else does.

He lifts his finger, telling me to wait. He comes back very quickly, holding an iPhone. He hands it to me.

"For you."

I don't get it. Why me? Then I get this odd feeling. It

starts in the pit of my stomach and moves up to my throat, making it difficult for me to speak. "Me?"

"Yes. His phone. Natasha, she come here, she say, everything in the Notes is you. So you must read."

"But where is he?"

"He always know you will come for caffé. He just don't know when."

Where is he? I'm here!

He shakes his head. His shoulders droop like he's carrying all the quota of sadness allocated to everyone living in the world. "He come down from office. He come here, we think . . . walk always . . . for his caffé . . . He forget this phone in office, he turn, we think, but that horrible van come crashing."

The fear cells inside me stand at fierce attention, making it hard for me to swallow or listen. I am straining to hear what he's saying—I'm praying it's the thick accent and the lack of vocabulary that's making him say what I think he's saying. Everything sounds knotted up and jumbled and impossibly wrong. He sits down opposite me like it's an exhausting move to execute. He places the phone between us. I stare at it. He stares at me.

My hands are clutching the edge of the table because I am aware they are shaking. He places both his hands on mine.

Is it possible to feel a tsunami of emotions and feel nothing at the exact same time?

Is it possible to feel every single what if, maybe, if only, stab at your soul till you're incontrovertibly numb? Is it possible for your stomach to keep turning while your brain remains inert? I cannot remember how long we sat that way. Finally, Attilio picks up the phone, slides the screen open, clicks on something, and passes it to me.

It's the Notes app, opened on a note simply titled, Seat 7B.

Dear Seat 7B,

It's been a year of Wednesdays since I asked you to meet me at Attilio's for the best espresso in the world. You said no, in the way only you can—a long, heartfelt speech without really saying the word no.

Also, it's been a year of Wednesdays since I walked out of that airplane cabin, without looking back. I was out of JFK and in my limo in less than twenty minutes. Perfect. Only it wasn't. The only thing harder than walking away is not looking back.

Let me tell you why.

I've had fifty conversations with you even before you wake up. I wake up before most people do—occupational hazard. Even though it's mostly contentious, finishing a conversation with you is like breathing. Like the twenty-eighth of February and the twenty-ninth of February, you remain this close and a year apart. I am afraid to wake up some mornings because I don't want to discover you're gone.

This person who talks, laughs (snorts), derides, argues, teaches, listens, asks and asks. And asks.

I've only met her once, about a year ago on a Wednesday in November. She believes all days are born equal, but some days are more equal than others. Wednesdays come with a halo. Nothing bad can happen on a Wednesday. She is a green warrior, but is missing a green thumb: she can kill a plant with love. She says coffee is an Aretha Franklin song, but drinks only tea. Masala tea. Rain! She can talk about it from one monsoon to the next and takes it personally if we think of it as bad weather. Nothing tears her up like watching the stars in a dark sky. Nothing soothes her like a jet trail in a bright blue sky. She may sign up for Musk's mission to Mars if only the guilt didn't weigh her down—carbon footprint :) She's learned that losing someone is always unfair. But being hugged by a stranger can heal you. She treasures lefties almost as much as she treasures the number three. She has some serious moxie: she may tell you to stop jerking yourself off when you aren't being the best version of yourself. She believes if her boys learn and teach kindness, her job is done. She says looking out for someone you love has to be the whole point of our existence—what else is there? If we can't do that, then at least we must live for hot, exploding-with-crunch jalebis. Or, four people and one dog squeezing into one bed. She dreams about Florence, but never plans on getting there. She wants to do little big things, but wishes she wasn't such a noticer. She loves Roger Federer because he is the cathedral of civility and she worships Grand Central like it's the Sistine Chapel. She's happy to turn into a criminal mastermind to save a child from missing a dead goldfish. She thinks the two most powerful words in the world are 'It's me'. Although, she wants to be remembered for the words 'She cared'. She doesn't want grand gestures. She only wants to make the stars sigh. If she loves you, she's going to stand by you. She believes if nobody wants to do what's right, what's good, then what's the point? If you can't be illogically good, uncomfortably good, if you can't be loyal when no one is looking . . . what's the point? She gives the longest explanations for the shortest questions. She never tires of asking questions. Like, 'Your greatest weakness?' I never answered that last one, so here goes. It's not being able to say the words: I need you.

Remember Jason? Wingman. Co-suffering childhood buddy. Bro. My responsibility. He didn't make it. Over-dosed. I did nothing. I had this constricting feeling in my chest as I sat on the steps in the main concourse of Grand Central and I thought about what you said: losing someone is always unfair. Sometimes, I am convinced you can hear me.

Natasha and I are no longer together. We

wanted different things. Well, you did say you should never have to tell someone how to love you. You also said love is too big and too hard to handle, love is also unbearably small, love is magnanimous, and on some days love just hides and can't be found. I don't know which it was. But Paris and New York were never the problem. Because how would you explain that you and I are tied in knots that even distance and absence cannot undo?

I start a new job in three weeks. No more big bad oil. You can finally stop looking at me like I just wrapped a string of explosives around Planet Earth and pressed the detonate button.

I watch a movie when I want to unwind, when I want to forget, when I want to remember. Last night I watched *City of Angels*. Again. An angel (Nick Cage) falls in love with a mortal (easy to do when the mortal is Meg Ryan). He gives up eternity to become human, just to be with her. I manage risk. I make money on risk (of course you know that and don't approve). I can tell you right off the bat that the risk was just not worth taking. And yet, I give Nick the highest of fives for doing what he did. Spoiler alert, they still don't get together. What stuck with me was that one line: I don't understand a God who would let us meet, if there's no way we could ever be together. I can't lie, I cry at the movies. Now that I've displayed an impressive lack of chill, I'll just move on.

Knowing you is like knowing a fictional character—you're not really there. But you're everywhere. You show up in my thoughts. You also show up in the spaces between my thoughts. I finish pending arguments with you when I should be talking to a real, live person in front of me. Here's the problem: I seem to be searching for you in everyone I meet. Maybe, just maybe, if we meet, everything will get recalibrated and I'll go back to being me before I met you.

Can we meet at Attilio's next Wednesday? I know you can hear me. I know you'll come. Because I just looked out of the window and saw the perfect jet trail streak across the sky.

I know how much you love your life and everyone in it. It's the best thing about you. I would never want that to change. I just need you in my head like a traveller needs a compass: to lean to my authentic north. Just be there. I need your grace.

If you don't show up before the credits roll then I know this: we will meet in another story. And when we do, it'll be my chance to say your two favourite words: It's me.

I'll end with your favourite sign because one way or another, there is more to come

—

I feel numb. I feel deaf. I feel absolutely nothing. Even my heart seems to have stopped beating. And then without warning, I can hear the sounds from the street outside— only, they're amplified a million-fold. A muddled cacophony of ear-ravaging sounds. My stomach lurches into my chest, which feels like it's going to explode. Is this what a heart seizure feels like? Or is this what astonishing pain feels like? I can feel everything. I begin to feel every loss I've ever felt seeping through my skin into my bones. I hug myself. I need to make sure my limbs are all intact. I should not be aching like an amputee. Not for someone I've met just once in my life. I hear an anguished sob, I don't realize it's from me until Attilio hands me a white handkerchief. An old-fashioned white handkerchief like my father always carried.

He places a small white cup of coffee in front of me. It's an espresso. Seat 7A's espresso. I sip it. It's hot. It's bitter. It's sweet. It burns my throat. Coffee should be black as hell, strong as death, and sweet as love. Those were my lines, but I can see Seat 7A smiling his camera flash smile as he delivers them back to me. He has his jacket hooked on his thumb, slung over his back, he's going to leave but this time he turns back, "One helluva plot twist, huh?" Fade to black.

I finish my first-ever cup of espresso. I reach for his phone and tell him everything I need to.

—

Born and raised in Kolkata, Sonia has lived and worked in Chennai, Mumbai, Delhi, Jakarta, Miami, Brussels, Johannesburg, and Singapore. With home being everywhere and nowhere, her belief in the power of the moment became a religion. An affirmation that unexpected and undeniable human connections are everything. Meanwhile, on the work front, she spent a huge chunk of her life, her days, and sleepless nights, in advertising—writing ads for all things from coffee and cars to condoms and candy—while dreaming of morphing 30-second commercials to full-length feature films. Not surprisingly, she threw caution, and her full-time job as creative director, to the winds and embarked on a riveting rejection-filled screenwriting journey in the US. Finally her day job entails writing movies! In a recent, delightful plot twist, her debut novel, *The Spectacular Miss*, was optioned by a leading Bollywood studio and she was commissioned to write the screenplay.

Sonia writes and re-writes in Singapore where she lives with her menagerie: gorgeous itinerant daughter, honorary proofreader husband, and her made-for-the-movies golden retriever, Ari Gold.